Pieces of Her Life

Pieces of Her Life

by G.C. Tindley

ISBN: 978-0-9996746-5-9
Library of Congress Control Number: 2019938793

Designed and Published by:
The Solid Foundation Group, LLC
www.TheSolidFoundationGroup.com

Printed in the United States of America

Acknowledgements

It wouldn't be right if I didn't first thank God for giving me this special gift and for allowing me to create so freely. I'd also like to thank The Solid Foundation Group for not only believing in me, but for also paving the way for my first project to go from dream to reality.

Next, I'd like to acknowledge and thank my mother, Jacqueline, who instilled "education first," and who always made me use the dictionary. You are where I got the love for words from.

A special thanks to: Drea, for showing me how to write in cursive and for helping me with my homework; to my cousin and cheerleader (from day one), Javon Walker…thank you for always keeping me on track…I love you; and, to my best friends, Chere McNabb and Deja Withers, I appreciate your patience during this journey and for always keeping me going.

To all my past lovers who broke my heart, thank you, as well! It's because of you all that I have such great stories to tell.

And, last, but not least, a special thanks goes to my spirit animal, Mady Tep, who has been my motivation when I felt like giving up.

Dedication

I dedicate my first book to my first love:
Devon Dancray Rice – the reason for all of my diary entrees.

May you continue to rest in peace
as my memories of you last forever.

Introduction

I often wonder why God chose me to go through hell and back. Maybe so that if I were strong enough to survive, I could tell my story and help others just like myself?! Sounds pretty easy when you actually say it out loud huh? Well nothing about how my life seemed to change overnight was easy. What I know for sure, is that everything happens for a reason and if it weren't for getting pregnant at 16, running away and forced into prostitution I wouldn't be standing before you today.

Like many of us, we had dreams and a well thought plan of how we wanted our lives to be. Some of us followed a straight and narrow path while others of us took the wrong turns, ran into dead end streets, or ended up in a different state. Perhaps you ran out of gas and never made it to your destinations at all. There was a point in my life where I thought I would never get out, see my life as I always imagined. You see both of my parents were professionals. My dad was a dentist for over 25 years and mom a teacher, so I knew at a early age I too was going to be something great.

I've always been good at helping people work through there problems, so naturally I knew by high school I was going to be a psychologist. But like half of teenagers in the world I got caught up in how cute boys were and one caught my attention, and in turned fell in love and of course pregnant.

I chose to be rebellious and not listen to my parents because I wanted to be captain of my own ship. I was sent away to a boarding school to hide my pregnancy, and to not shame the Porter name. But I had plans of my own.

I ran away to avoid my baby being adopted and as a result I ended up far, far away from home. I turned to prostitution, not by choice but force by someone I thought I could trust. Although not happy about that time in my life, I took what I went through and flipped it for the better.

I got my GED, took the untouched money I saved from having sex with dirty, strange men and enrolled in college, and the rest is history.

"I really hope my story has inspired you all today, and enjoy my first of many books, as I continue to heal and work with the youth and adults of our community. It's been fifteen years since my roller coaster journey began and I'm just getting started. Thank you all for coming out, please enjoy the food and great music".

In the corner of the room I set up a booth for people to do a meet and greet with me, and for me to sign my book for them. My wonderful baby daddy, and star basketball player even set up for the press to come out to add some exposure.

Eastside Long Beach Chick

Palm trees,
Summer breeze,
in these mean streets of Long beach.
Dope boys,
Lo- riders, dime bags
and Bean pies sold in front of the V.I.P.
I'm from the city where we throw house parties,
kids eating jujubes, and sunflower seeds.
Another body dead in a ditch
because somebody snitched.
BBQ's and daisy dukes going up at Kings Park,
all for the love and the city of the LBC!!!

After my seminar I had a driver that Demoni insisted I have take me to meet up at Barbette's (with my closest friends and family) to continue the celebration. Most writers have seminars, speaking engagements and book signings to promote their books which is one marketing tool that helps get their name out there better. Being that I've never done anything like this before I was both excited and nervous. Thanks to dear old dad he was here to guide me through this entire process. For the first time people get to see me up close and personal, someone whose dealt with the chaos of prostitution; raising a child as a single parent, trying to date like normal a normal person and a hint of professionalism.

I wanted this seminar to uplift and inform people that Tracy Porter is not perfect and yet with all my knowledge and degrees I too have issues but together we can work it out.

I welcomed everyone out, from teachers to single parents, community leaders, readers of nonfiction, inspiring writers and those perhaps looking for help.

During intermission I read excerpts of my book to give people a taste of what I do. And with the time I had left over I answered questions. I even had a few clients of mine who agreed to share their stories similar to the topic covered in the seminar. It was also at my seminar that I announced that I was expanding my services to help more people who maybe couldn't afford the prices for therapy. The crowd of people who came out were so happy to hear I was now going to be providing free group sessions for those in need, regardless of the different types of issues they may have. After a few hugs, pictures, email exchanges and autograph signings I was ready to go and unwind!

It was on my ride with my driver Mark that I reflected on the event; the crowd's responses, and how lives may have changed from the words I spoke. Being that the book hadn't been out that long I was surprised at how many attendees already had the book. I even chuckled a few times because there were times I added extra things in to prove a point during my storytelling.

As we were cruising down Pacific Coast Highway, my phone rang. Demoni Thomas! A good old blast from the past a.k.a. my baby daddy that I will forever be grateful for. "What's up, babe?"

"Hey you!"

"You did a great job tonight, I'm so proud of you Tracy."

Demoni, was a tall brown skin dude who I dated my ninth and tenth grade year in high school and then briefly after getting out of jail. For six months this dude would low key follow me to my classes, and at first I thought it was a coincidence.

Until one day my girl Selasi gave me a note with the pound sign with number 21 on it, a boy's' name and contact number. The last thing I was concerned about were boys when I was too busy making sure I could remember where all my classes were.

"Aye ,Tee, Demoni told me to give you his number and for you to call him."

I had no idea that the guy who followed me was the same person who gave me his number at first but I knew he either was a football or basketball player based on his height. Instead of asking her more questions I jammed the note in my back pocket and headed to my next class.

One day I was walking to third period heading to Mr. Lobliner's math class, (*which I hated*) I suddenly felt a huge arm around my frail shoulders. Although I was a tall girl, this person towered over me like a skyscraper.

"Sup, Shawty? I'm going to walk you to your class, Tee, right?"

I was nervous and pissed all at the same time. I mean who just walks up on people like that! I stopped, looked him square in the eye and said my name is Tracy and only people who know me can call me Tee.

I picked up the pace because as much as I hated math I didn't like being late, otherwise I would have to report to OCS with Ms. Cook and I heard she was mean as hell.

"Aight then, little mama, I'll talk to you later." I looked back at Demoni, rolled my eyes and mouthed loud enough for me to hear it, "I sure hope not."

After lunch and two periods later, I'm in Spanish class where a group of guys walked passed being all loud and obnoxious, and girls giggling. So naturally I wanted to see what was funny and to my surprise it was Demoni dancing at the door, showing off with some donuts in one hand and basketball tucked under his armpits. It was at that moment I figured out #21 was his jersey number for the basketball team.

I also realized at that moment just how fine he was and I could not stop staring at him, unlike earlier that morning. Then out of nowhere Mrs. Largo called me out. Embarrassed now because I was surprised and not prepared to answer the question, IN SPANISH.

?Buenas tarde senora? said Ms. Largo.

Instead of answering the question, my attention was still at the door where Demoni winked at me and blew me a kiss. OMG, if there was ever a moment when I wanted to hide under a rock that was it.

My body was on fire and I swear I sweated out my perm that day as well. It took a week to finally call him because I was not allowed to date until I was sixteen and I was only fourteen. Dad didn't say I couldn't have friends so until I could persuade him differently Demoni would have to be a friend.

I told no one but my first sexual attempt was an epic fail. Not sure why I was thinking about our first encounter. Maybe because I can't believe how far we've both come or maybe simply because one never forgets about their first love. Out of the blue I started laughing, boy we use to do some silly shit.

Going back to 1996 I can remember how Demoni and I planned for weeks to have sex, but had to shut the operation down after daddy found me and Demoni kissing on the front porch. He practically grounded me for life! Not really, but I had to go weeks with no extracurricular activities, or access to my phone which was pure evil. And to make matters worse my sister got to do whatever she wanted to but little did my parents know she was just as rebellious as me, if not more.

"You sure you want me to pop your cherry?" Trying to hide the roller coaster ride in my stomach I said as sweet as I could "hmmm mmm."

"You said you love me, right?" Chewing my gum all easy like New-New from the movie *ATL.*

"Yeah, boo, you know I do."

I was oblivious to all the signals of bullshit then. Demoni was saying everything I wanted to hear yet never gazing into my eyes, but what did I know at 14/15. After his lies and charming ways of sweet nothings, we quickly kissed each other goodbye and headed to our next class before anyone saw us. But not after being caught by miss cock blocker who shall remain nameless.

After telling the girls my plan they were super excited because I would officially become a woman and we could finally compare notes. My sister was totally against it and warned me about every bad possible situation that could happen.

Being she's so extreme, she said if Mama caught me, she would send me away for good and I would no longer be a part of the family.

"Are you sure you want to do this? I mean what's the rush? Demoni ain't got a cute bone in his body."

I rolled my eyes and tossed my hair back.

"Don't hate, he said he loved me."

My sister laughed at me like I was a comedian on Def Jam.

"That's what all the boys say to girls when they want to do the nasty, even I know that."

As conflicted as I was, I had to see what all the hype was about. Now, years later I can laugh at how dumb I was and how I wish I'd listened to my sister. But when you're in love nothing no one says can make you change your mind.

I remember like it was yesterday. The plan was to leave campus on lunch and go to his house since mom did after school tutoring on Wednesday and dad was always at the office late. So I didn't have to worry about being caught. On our walk there, I swear it took forever even though it was only five minutes from the school. I was beyond nervous but was too afraid to change my mind out of fear he would end up dumping me on sight.

So, I played it cool and went ahead anyway. I noticed how clean his room was when we walked in, which meant he must have made it extra special just for me. He turned on his little boom box next to the window, drew the shades and told me he'd be right back. I took my backpack off my shoulders, slipped off my shoes and sat on the edge of the bed.

Then when he re-entered the room, he had two glasses of E&J brandy in some mason jars. After just a few sips I become relaxed, ears ringing loud and palms sweating just like the day he walked past my Spanish class a few months back. He took off his shoes, cap and sweatshirt he often wore on days we had rallies. We were sitting so close to each other I swear he could hear my heartbeat but I knew he couldn't, it was just me being paranoid.

He then cupped my chin with his palm, drew his lips toward mine and we kissed heavily, our breaths smelling like liquor. After sucking on my earlobes he whispered in my ears, "Just relax, baby."

Just when I was getting ready to get to the good part my phone rang, and it was my mother wanting me to give her a recap of the event since she and dad couldn't make it to the book signing. Dad just had knee surgery and since he would be both sedated and unable to drive, mom was by his side like she always had. I have to give my mom credit for sticking it out with dad during the years of infidelity. A lot of women after learning their husbands were cheating would have left them but not Roberta. As private as both my parents were, my sister, and I always knew when trouble was brewing in the household but like children we stayed in our place. Grown folks' business was just that, their business.

After getting off the phone with mom I went back strolling down memory lane. Damn I loved me some Demoni and couldn't anyone tell me shit. I thought I was grown after losing my virginity and I thought I had him right where I wanted him. What I really was, was a silly bitch headed for destruction. Yep I was fifteen, in high school and pregnant because my ass let a nappy headed boy talk me out my panties I didn't even buy. Fuck, my sister was right, I didn't have the good sense that God gave me. If I thought I was in trouble before, what I was about to reveal just took the cake.

The first person to notice any change in me was Nivea. As much as we fought, we knew everything about one another.

"So, what's up T, you've been in the bathroom every twenty minutes for the last hour."

I looked at her like she was a crazy person asking her why she was clocking my every move and that I was looking for my hair brush. She laughed explaining that 1st off I had braids and second, if that was the case then why did I close the door each time.

I tried to think fast, but I had nothing. She grabbed me by the arm pulling me into her room and locked it before saying another word.

"So, you pregnant, huh?"

Not sure what to say, but I was late getting my period which is a sure sign of being with child.

"We always get our period at the same time, and I noticed you didn't. Plus, when you undressed the other day, I couldn't help but see how dark your nipples were,"

"What the fuck Niv? how do you know all of this you're just an 8th grader? And why are looking at my body perv?"

The look she gave me was let me know I was caught, and I was going to need her help big time. I was smart when it came to the books but I wasn't so bright for being street smart.

"It's called school silly, and I pay attention to things and my womanly instincts say you are prego, Sista!"

I cried because sooner or later I would have to decide and tell all parties involved. Nivea and I made a pack we'd pretend this conversation never happened and go on about the day as normal. Sounded like a great plan except for one thing. MOM! Either I was starving that night or nervous because I pigged out "Ma, you put your foot in these greens!"

"They are bomb, huh?"

"Umm, Dad, please stop trying to be hip."

We all laughed at the efforts my dad was doing to stay current with two teenage daughters. Even mom laughed, but there was something in her eyes that told me she was hunting for something.

"Nivea, can you wash the dishes tonight while I talk to Tracy?"

"But Ma, it's her night. Ugh…. Fine, whatever."

I've never been burned before but right now I was in front of a blazing fire and mom was burning me. Nivea picked up on the vibe as well and to make sure she wasn't next she hurried to the kitchen. As for me when even I was about to get talked to I knew better than to move or say a word. My dad asked if he needed to be excused, and without looking at him she calmly said, "No, you stay."

Being that my dad was a typical man, he did not understand what was about to go down.

"So. should I start, or do you want to first?" I wasn't sure if that was a trick question or not, so in between long gulps of my soda I told mama I'd let her go first especially since I wasn't sure what the talk was about and under no means was I going to incriminate myself.

Mom told me how she received a phone call while at work that I had been skipping classes. What seemed to be nothing at first since I was never late or absent from the first day I began school, EVER!! Once in fourth grade I had a terrible cold, and I kept telling my parents I was fine knowing I was up all night coughing and running a temp.

Against my mom's judgement I talked her into letting me attend school because I couldn't be a success in the bed. So off to school I went, until after lunch time, when the nurse came to get me from Mr. Heath's class due to falling asleep during SSR.

Since my mom was a teacher, she couldn't abandon her class, so she sent dear ole dad to get me. She instructed him to give me a cold bath to help break my fever, rub Vicks all over my chest, make me put on socks and get under the covers only showing my eyes. The other thing I could do was watch cartoons until mom came home to take over.

I got in trouble for skipping class, and dad just looked at me, not saying a word. Then mom told me to go to my room and wait. Like Nivea she too noticed I didn't get my period, especially since she bought our feminine products. "So how late are you?"

"Huh…maaaaam?"

"Don't fucking maaaaam me, Tracy. You let that nappy headed ass boy get you pregnant and you think I wouldn't notice?" I was young once myself and I've been pregnant twice so I know the score."

My mouth hit the floor because mom never cussed and I'm almost sure I peed on myself when she busted in my room. Right away I cried, telling her I didn't know how far along and, yes, I was having sex and that was the reason I skipped so many days of class for the last three months.

"So instead of telling your father, together we'll go see Dr. Reuben."

Okay was all I could muster.

"Now wash your dirty face and help Niv with whatever dishes she has left."

I tried to move in for a hug and mom knowing me all too well, she pushed me away from her in disgust. For the first time in my life I felt unwanted and ashamed and knew then that I never wanted to feel that way to my parents or anyone I loved.

Mom planned the abortion perfectly. It was spring break, which meant no missed school days, Dad would be busy at the office so my procedure would be done without him questioning. My sister was also made to go so that if she ever thought about having unprotected sex and came home pregnant, she too would be punished. I was also told not to tell Demoni out of fear of he and his food stamp receptionist of a mother possibly wanting the baby. My mom's words, not mine. Plus, the last thing I wanted was for my reputation to be tarnished.

After that first time of being broken in, we had sex almost every day we had a chance to. We did it in the morning before school, after school when basketball practice was over, and during lunch. Our not returning back to school is how I got in trouble because the school called my mother. Man, the things we did I would not want my daughter to know and pray to God she won't repeat what I did until she is ready, or better yet married!!

Now let me fast forward some. My heart was beating so fast 1, 2, 3, 4, 5. 1, 2, 3, 4, 5. Right before I peed on myself the doctor informed us that the procedure was not going to take place because I was too far along in my pregnancy. Not to mention that I was too young and it would be too much for my body to take on. "Thank you, God," I said to myself and then my stomach fluttered. I was in love, and just when I was just about to jump for joy I looked into my mother's eyes.

She was furious as a steam pot. I swear I seen smoke come out of her ears. Mom's brain was already brewing and plan B was going to be planned out by the time we reached the car. It was dead silent during the drive home and no one even so much breathed. The only thing my mother said was, "Now I have to tell your father. Dammit it, Tracy!"

I thought that aborting my baby was gonna be the worst thing that ever happened in my life until my parents decided I would be attending an all-girls Boarding School in Pasadena to have the baby. Then my baby would be given up for adoption. WTF!! Moreover, I was no longer going to be daddy's princess.

I cried for the rest of the day. How was I to tell Demoni, and furthermore how was I going to explain that he and I could no longer be together or even friends? From that moment on I was forever changed, and this was the start of my many experiences about boys, men and how the world worked.

Although I didn't really look pregnant yet, I was sent away during my fifth month to a city away from family and friends to a school called Westwood Boarding School. It was set up specially for defiant girls ranging from age ten to seventeen, because once a person was 18, by law they had to let them go. I almost wished I was able to abort my baby because I wouldn't have been sent to this miserable place. These girls were over the top spoiled, and some stupid for no reason, who got into trouble just because.

This girl name Catalina got kicked out of 6 schools within the past year for fighting all because her mother remarried. She wanted badly to live with her real father. Tania was arrested for stealing clothes at Fifth Saks so she could pay for drugs for the wannabe rapper boyfriend. I was among dozens of other girls who were pregnant and sent here because our families didn't want to be shamed.

The youngest pregnant girl was 12. She was raped by her uncle but no one believed her, so she was sent away as punishment.

Most of my time there was a blur. Everyone was a part of a clique already and I just wanted to sleep all day but wasn't allowed to, due to chores I had to do when my last class was over. I do remember throwing myself into my Creative Writing and Art class because I could express myself without anyone controlling how I held the paint brush or how to tell my story. There were no phones allowed and I was missing Demoni like crazy. My last week home before coming to Westwood Academy Demoni and I had to tell his parents the news about my pregnancy, but what they didn't know was that I was being forced to give the baby up. Mom and Dad feared that the Thomas's family would fight for custody. My family wanted the problem to go away. Period! He could tell I was avoiding him or hiding something, so he called me out one day after my dance class.

"So, you gonna keep walking past me like you don't see my big ass. What's wrong, did I do something?"

Not ready for this conversation I did what any girl would do, I cried uncontrollably making no sense at all. Totally freaking him out, he hugged and planted small kissed on my forehead until I calmed down. Damn he smelled so good. I had to tell myself that I had to focus because it was because of these embraces that got my ass pregnant in the 1st place.

"Demoni we can't ever see each other anymore. My parents forbid me to have any contact with you while living under their roof."

He cocked his head to the side, stepped back and asked me why. He began reciting to me that everything would be fine and that he was going to ask his mom Ms. Beverly if I can move in so we can raise our baby together.

"They can't do that, Tee. I love you baby. I don't understand how they even found out since we've been so good at keeping quiet."

I sighed long and hard because I knew I couldn't lie to him, even though I was going to break his heart and I was risking the possibility of him hating me forever.

"Before you get angry or say something you can't take back, just hear me out."

"Okay."

"Mom got a call from the school about me skipping class and she knew I missed my period."

"Aight, go on, shorty."

"Now, I'm being sent to a boarding school where I will remain until I have the baby."

Damn, there was that hatred look again. Demoni stopped me in mid-sentence in what appeared to be tears, and said, "So, what does that mean for me and my family, Tracy. Don't we have a say?"

"I know you're mad, but try to see that my parents are trying to protect me?"

"Protect you? You mean they don't want to be the laughing stock of their bougie ass friends. It's not about you at all, boo, don't you see?"

I was in full on tears because I was afraid to tell him that when I got back I'd be without our baby. Clearly Demoni had enough of my not making sense so his last words to me were, "You know what, fuck you and your family!"

I was stunned by his words because just a few seconds ago he was professing his love for me and now it was fuck me, and he wasn't exactly quiet about it either. I tried to explain to him how I didn't want to do it but didn't see any other options. How would we support a baby with no jobs and barely a high school diploma?

"I see."

"So, you understand why this is goodbye?"

"No, and I'll never forgive your mother for sending you away. We could have worked something out, since I "DO" plan to make it to the NBA after college, our lives will be set for life."

Before walking away from me, he gave me one last kiss on the forehead and never looked back. From that day forward, I had to walk around pretending Demoni and I never met. You know how hard that was for me, being that I was carrying his child? It would be a long time before I ever trusted a guy again and nothing he could say or do would trick me out my panties again unless I choose to.

For years after that I resented my parents, my mother more because she called the shots in just about every damn situation. They should have been supportive and provided us with guidance because Demoni and I should have been able to choose what to do with our baby.

After all it was our responsibility not theirs, but as usual Mom was so busy trying to paint the perfect picture of our family when we're really faking the funk like most people we knew.

Once my Dad knew what was going on, he couldn't believe what was going on in his house and ignored my mother for weeks because she made decisions without consulting him first. It was also the first time I seen my father cry. And although he was beyond disappointed in me, he told me I was still his little princess. I would never forget that, as long as I live.

"Tracy, I can't believe you threw away your life for a little piece of dick. Was my love and affection not enough?"

Crying non-stop, with boogers rolling down my face and all I could do was apologize repeatedly. "I know, Dad, and I'm sorry." He just walked away with his head down in disappointment with his hands in his pockets.

Flipped Inside Out

What do you want to be when you grow up?
A doctor? a lawyer? a nurse?
All of that, and not a soul
told me to beware of the thirst.
A trap that kidnaps your innocence.
And,
One bad decision and your life is ruined.
Forever!!

Sometimes being a psychologist is great. Other times it's a bitch, because although I service those with emotional, behavioral, physical trauma and relationship problems I struggle with my own demons. All I've ever wanted was to be dangerously in love like mama and daddy, have a great career and travel the world with my friends. But I had to go through being pregnant before I was ready, being taken advantage of and abused by a pimp. Also, being split up from my daughter while in jail and literally having to start my life all over.

Although I now wear my crown on straight, I've been embarrassed for years by my actions. And retelling my story is never easy. Oh, and let's forget about dating! My girls say I'm so picky, that I scare men away with my book smarts and street credibility, lol. What's wrong with that, every woman wants a challenge, and wants to be taken serious right? But the way my life twisted and turned I now know how to weed out the bull shitters from the serious inquiries with my eyes closed.

As it got closer to my due date, the bigger I became. I excelled in school because I refused to let my situation be a setback to success. I was very tired and cranky I think because I was alone and wanted my baby more than anything in life. Me and baby girl already had a bond and to lose that didn't sit well with me. One day I got a call during class for me to report to the main school office because I had an important call from my parents. I thought that was strange.

Since they only called once every Sunday so and it was in the middle of the day during the week something must have been wrong. After I wobbled to the office and catching my breathe, I said hello to a voice I'd never thought I would hear again.

"Demoni!!"

"Hey, baby, how did you know what school I was at."

"Your sister, Nivea, and I talked and she told me everything. Runaway with me."

As compelling as that sounded, I didn't want to be selfish. He had college scouts looking to recruit him and I know basketball was his life and I didn't want to mess any chances of him being successful because of our screw up.

"Demoni, I love you with all my heart. The baby and I will be fine. College is where you will go, and when the time is right, we'll be together."

He was dead silent soaking up everything I just said and as much as he hated to be wrong, I knew he was going to thank me later.

"Tracy as much as I feel we can do this I think you might be right."

I was in tears of happiness and sadness. Later on that night I heard a tap on my window, and it was Demoni. He said he had to see me and touch my belly to connect with the baby. I told him that I was busting out this nutty place they called school after Sydney was born.

"So, it's a girl?"

He was all smiles as he touched me and kissing me all over. I was becoming aroused and wanted to take him in the closet I shared with my roommate and have sex with him.

He gave me that look like he knew what I was thinking, so I pulled him closer to me and into the closet that wasn't that spacious and my belly didn't make it any better but I didn't care. Not sure if the baby could feel any of what we were doing but I had to have him and wasn't worried about getting into trouble. It was after that night, that I had decided that after I gave birth I was going to escape. All I needed was the perfect plan and help from one of the girls at the school I could trust. The following weekend my family came to see me. Nivea and I hugged it out like Celie and Netty did at the end of *The Color Purple*.

Dad was in a brighter mood than he had been since all this mess began. He wouldn't stop kissing me and touching my belly. He asked how his two princesses we're doing and that he missed me so much being at the house and how my friends came by looking for me.

Mommy dearest then slid in telling me how she came up with a clever story, and blah blah blah. Dad and Nivea just rolled their eyes and sighed as she drained us about this and that.

"Oh, by the way Tracy we found two lovely families who are interested in adopting the baby."

She showed me their files and asked me which one I preferred so that the baby can be placed with the right family. Wow, she was allowing me to have control of that?

"You are carrying the baby well, and should snap back in no time. How is school?"

"Fine, mother, I guess...just want to have a healthy baby and get back to my normal life."

"That's good, dear, we can't wait to be one big happy family like we once were before...well, you know."

Before the mood got sour Dad took over again asking me what I was going to name the baby and all that jazz and had I started thinking about college. Right before they left, I had my one on one time with Nivea. I thanked her for keeping Demoni abreast of what was going on. told her how he came to see me a few nights before and my plans to escape with the baby. She promised to keep the secret and if I needed her again for anything else that she would come running. My mom even managed to hug me but only because I had six weeks to go and she was happy that she'd have her daughter back. But what she didn't know was that I was not playing her fucking games anymore.

Considering I was young and pregnant, my pregnancy was pretty breezy up until the last few weeks. My feet were beyond swollen so much that I could barely wear shoes. I couldn't feel my vagina and everyone was getting on my damn nerves.

My mom was calling every fucking day telling me how excited Mr. and Mrs. Robertson were about finally having a baby of their own and that I was their blessing. While I listened, I breathed in and out slowly as my contractions have been coming on stronger and stronger.

"Tracy, are you okay?"

"Yes, Mom, the baby is due soon and I've been super tired lately and having contractions."

I could hear my parents talking about it's almost time and how they needed to get a hold of the Robertson's because Sydney's arrival was nearing.

"Margaret, calm down, before you pass out."

I chuckled, because I could totally see my mother doing the most and my dad trying to keep her overly dramatic ass in check.

"Baby girl, are you okay? Do you need us to come take you to the hospital?"

"No, Daddy, I'm fine. It's just a little contraction. Nothing to be concerned about, yet."

A few weeks back my roommate Claudia and I had become like best friends. I helped her with her English Comp class and she helped plan the perfect getaway. She got a hold of her boy Tyrone, who had a friend who was willing to let me crash at his place until I figured out my next step. Since it was less traffic during the weekend I would leave then, almost unnoticed.

"So. Tyrone's friend, Vinny, will be the one to pick you and the baby up out back of the hospital where he will drive you both to Sacramento where Caleb lives."

"Caleb? What kind of name is that?"

"I don't know girl and anyways who cares. No one will expect to look for you there and since no one ever sees us talking to one another I too will go under the radar far as being questioned."

As nervous as I was, I was excited as well. As long as the plan worked that is. I asked that I spend at least a week with Sydney so that I could breastfeed and bond with her a little. I made sure I got all the signatures required to make sure that my wish was honored. This was done to make sure that my plan would go smoothly in case a hiccup happened and we had to make some changes. And then on March the 23rd around 4pm my water broke. I was taken to the hospital that was near the school, my parents and sister met me for there for the birth of my baby. Everything sorta happened so fast that there was no time to tell Demoni. I was going to hear it later for sure, but once I was hooked up to the monitors and feet in position to push all I wanted was the baby to be out.

After 16 hours of labor Sydney Anaya Thomas finally made her debut and boy, was she pretty. I knew for sure I was not doing this again under no circumstances. That shit hurt like hell, my vagina will never be the same and I felt like I had been hit by a truck and was told I had to go back to work on the slave yard. What I found crazy was how my mom swooned over Sydney with joy, like a happy grandmother. Sydney connected to her Papa and aunty Nivea right away.

And even with what I was going to do in a few days this was not going to end the way I would have liked. The icing on the cake was when Demoni and Ms. Beverly came to see her. She was her daddies twin. After everyone left, I broke down because the next 72 hours were crucial to my survival.

I pretended for the next few hours. But the twist was that my parents were soon going to find out that their plan for the baby to be adopted was not going to happen. And although Demoni knew I wanted to run away with the baby, he didn't know it would be up north with some stranger. Then my sister Nivea had to play it cool as she was the only one in on the real story, besides Claudia of course.

I was given the full description of the type of Van that was coming to pick me up, what Vinny looked like and to not say a word until it was safe. Although I was eager to get out the hospital, I was nervous as well, being with a complete stranger with my baby. All sorts of crazy things came to my head but If I were going to be a big girl this was the risk I had to take. Vinny was a scary ass dude. 6'5, several piercings on his face and a body filled with tattoos that's going to look nasty as he gets older. On the flip side of that, he was super nice. Not much of a talker. He did feed me, stopped whenever I had to use the restroom and was respectful whenever I needed to breastfeed Sydney.

It took half a day to drive to Sacramento. I was beyond tired and just wanted to get out the car and get a shower and sleep, plus baby girl was cranky. Vinny helped me to the door of my final destination. 2100 Fillmore Street, was a cute little one-story house on the corner that belonged to the person I would come to know very well. I knocked a few times, and then a door slowly opened.

"What's up, bro?", asked Vinny.

"What's up, my nigga?" said a gorgeous man with braids, wearing a wife beater and some khaki shorts.

I had to blink several times to soak in the beauty that stood before me. I had no idea who the man was at first, but what I did know was that he was all that and then some.

"Are you gonna come in, little mama, or nah?"

Not sure what to say at first, he took Sydney who was still in the car seat, took her out as if she were his.

After the initial shock I cleared my throat, "Um, my name is Tracy and that's my baby, Sydney".

Before I could proceed, he told me he knew all about me and that he was expecting my arrival. "By the way, I'm Caleb, but most people around here call me C Dubb."

"Oh, ok...nice to finally meet you, and thank you for taking me and my baby in."

"No problem, Ma."

Caleb gave me a tour of the house that I later found out was passed down to him from his late grandparents. The drive had been extremely long so I asked where my room was so that I could get a little shut eye. Every time I'd close my eyes, I replayed what happened and was still in shock that we were able to pull it off. I owed Claudia and Tyrone big time.

While I was in the hospital Claudia packed all my belongings so that when I gave her the green light everything would be good to go. Once my family left to go back to Long Beach I texted her to say that I was going to be in the hospital for just one more day just to make sure that me and the baby were ok. Once I was discharged I was to go back to the school to be with Sydney the remainder of the week before I handed her off. The day I was released I was both nervous and excited because I had no idea what was going to happen, once I fled.

Not sure how long I was sleep for; but, when I woke I panicked and was discombobulated. I looked all around the room for Sydney thinking someone had taken her, just to run into the other room with her once again in Caleb's arms.

"I didn't want to disturb you. She was crying so I made her a bottle".

"I see, Well, thank you sir".

"Call me Caleb".

"Ok, Caleb. How do you know so much about babies?"

"I have two of my own, so I've had some practice", he said followed by a giggle. Damn he sure was sexy with his wife beater and khakis on. "You don't mind, do you?" Once again staring at him I tried to be normal in my reply. "Oh no, not at all. You've been more than helpful and I don't want to burden you with my responsibilities."

He smiled at me, kissed me on the forehead then placed Sydney on my lap. "She is beautiful."

I thanked him and couldn't help but think of Demoni because she was a mirror image of her father. Which at that moment reminded me that I needed to check in with Nivea, so I sent her a text message with Caleb's number on it and for her to call. I also gave her the address just in case I was in danger she knew where to have my parents find me.

"You must be hungry?"

And boy was I. Not only was Caleb fine as wine he was also a pretty good cook. We had fried chicken, macaroni and cheese, mash potatoes and corn bread. Over dinner we had small talk, and since I was much younger than he was my stories were short and sweet. Later that night the phone rang and it was my sister, and boy was I happy to hear her voice. She told me she had to wait until my parents were asleep before she called me. She asked me about the baby, the drive and whether or not I was ok. I assured her that everything was fine and to pretend she knew nothing and that I would call her in a few days. We talked and texted just about every other day for the first 6 months but then after sometime the calls stopped completely, then the text messaging.

Young, Sprung and Dumb

The first year in Sacramento with Caleb was everything a young girl could dream of. He kept me laced with my hair and nails done. Shopping for me and Syd every week, and the places we would dine were upscale. I went from being a guest to being his main squeeze. We sorta fell in a routine of being lovers almost quickly. At first, we were just friends learning one a another but that's how the game had to be worked. Anything I needed I got. He taught me all the skills I use on the men I frequented with from oral sex, to my slick talk and how I take pipe. One thing I didn't do was anal.

I remember the 1st time Caleb and I were intimate. I was even more nervous than I was when Demoni and I had sex. Probably because he and I were kids and Caleb was a grown ass man. I was sixteen and he was twenty-eight at the time. I had only been with one person so I knew this was going to be a teachable moment. I had just given baby girl a bath, fed her one last time and put her to bed and had anticipated doing the same. Wrong! Caleb was looking at me in a way he hadn't before. I was somewhat nervous and even looked around as if someone else was there because there was no way he was eyeing me like he was.

"Aye, you wanna finish watching this movie with me?"

"What you watching?"

"All About the Benjamins".

"Oh, ok sure. I was about to hit the hay but I guess I can wait".

He nodded at what I said pretending to be all into the movie. He took a swig of his 40 and a few puffs of his joint and passed it to me. I smiled a little bit, then kindly declined reminding him that I was breastfeeding.

"Oh yeah. My fault. I forgot, babe."

But it didn't stop there. He drew me in for a kiss that almost caused a waterfall. It's been over six months since I had my baby and the last time I was intimate was with Demoni in my room closet I shared with Claudia at the all-girls school I attended. I pushed back and tried to run to the room I occupied with Sydney.

"Where you going?"

"To my room. I don't feel right about this."

"Don't be scared, I know you know how to fuck."

I wanted to slap the shit out of him for saying that to me like I was all of a sudden, a slut.

"I'm sorry, I'm sorry. I didn't mean it like that, Tracy. I just meant..."

Not wanting to piss him off I told him it was okay and that I forgave him. We continued to watch the movie, which I don't know until this day why I didn't use this opportunity to go to my room and lock the door.

Thirty minutes later Caleb was at it again, this time he moved in closer to me on the sofa in a spooning position kind of. I scooted back toward him and arched my back some like a cat does. That was an open invitation for him to proceed and boy did he ever.

I just knew the dick was going to be bomb. He was a grown man. And a fine one at that! I know I shouldn't be having sex with a man twice my age or at all since being sexually active is how I got into this mess in the 1st place. But my curiosity got the best of me which is one reason I didn't go to my room when I had the chance. He planted small kisses on my neck first, my earlobes and then filled my small mouth making waves in my stomach like never before. Instead of fighting it I slowly began to let go and partook of the pleasure that Caleb had instore for me.

We migrated to his room and right away he got on top of me, taking off my pj bottoms and kissing me again. I raised my hands above my head to take off my top, looking at him watching him looking at me. He then took my now C cup breast and massaged them with his big hands, then inserted one into his mouth. Since I was lactating he drank some of the breast milk, which he liked all too well.

"Damn, Shawty, you taste good".

Lost for words I closed my eyes and moaned, not wanting to mess up the flow. Knowing that it was too late to turn back I blocked out all possible regrets, held onto his broad shoulders as he slowly entered my small pond.

Gasping for air at first as he began to thrust himself inside one inch at a time. Good lord he was big, I thought to myself. It was magical, like I was on a high I didn't want to come down from.

He went slowly, then picked up the tempo and I gladly rode the wave. It was that night I knew Caleb would be my drug of choice. My downfall and the reason I would ultimately get into serious trouble.

"You like daddy dick?"

"Yes." Shaking like a stripper.

Say it louder so I can hear you."

"Yes, daddy, I love this dick."

"Is this pussy mine?"

"Yes, it's yours, daddy. Oh shit, yes, yes, yes!"

We continued to make love for God knows how long. This was also the first time since giving birth to Sydney that she slept all night. Thank God.

The next morning after breakfast, "Do you love me?" he asked.

"Is that even a question? You already know the answer to that."

Caleb looked at me all sly and shit explaining to me how important it was for me to tell him how I felt about him in addition to showing him. We had been in Sacramento a year now and we were celebrating Sydney's 1st birthday. Oh how I wished my sister, my two best friends and parents were here to celebrate. Well, actually my dad. If my mother wouldn't have been set on hiding me and forcing me to give up my baby I wouldn't be in this mess. However, I was surrounded by Caleb and his people and a few of the neighbors who had small children.

I'm sure by now that Demoni hated everything about me. I lied to him, hid my plans of where I was running away to. But I also felt it was better this way because his future was important and I never wanted to get in the way of that.

Nor did I want him to resent me due to me becoming pregnant, so I guess in some way how things ended was meant to be. I did hate that my sister and I stopped talking, but that's life and one day I hope to reunite with her and thank her for being a ride or die and not ratting me out to my parents. Or did she? I mean we went from talking and texting almost every day to nothing at all.

As I sat eating my omelet, grits and bacon I went back in forth about my love and admiration for him. He and Sydney were busy making kissy faces and exchanging hugs. Sometimes when I look at her I get sad because it should be Demoni kissing his daughter and not Caleb. I had hoped as she got older, she'd take after me, but she didn't. Hell, she even had the same birthmark or her leg just like him. When I feel compelled to call him, I stop myself because if he knew where I was located, he would take Sydney away from me out of spite. I can't blame him, but my baby is my everything. I know that's selfish of me and he deserves every right to see his daughter but right now is not the right time.

It also didn't help that every time I've tried mentioning anything about home to Caleb, he said it's out of the question and he can provide a good life for me and Sydney like he's been doing.

"You're my girl now and don't you ever forget it."

When I'm not busy playing the mommy and wife roll, I sit on my bed and cry. I should have just done what my mother wanted me to do. I was missing out on my last two years of high school, all my friends, and I can forget about prom and graduation. I made a promise to myself one night when I could leave from Caleb's spell that I would get my G.E.D and go to college no matter how old I am when I accomplish my goals.

The last thing I wanted was to be an embarrassment to my daughter. I wanted to make her proud of me in spite of the journey I was on at the moment.

I remember being so down one day, feeling helpless and wishing I was home when my sister called me. Imagine the tears of joy that day. She explained to me that my parents had gotten suspicious asking all types of questions about my running away and if she knew where I was. She went on to say she denied having any involvement but once they checked her phone records she was busted. The school also got into big trouble because they were supposed to know where students were at all times and didn't understand how they let me slip away.

Every girl was interviewed and each provided them with nothing. I didn't talk to many of them and the one girl I did talk to was no longer there but even so Claudia was my bitch. She wasn't going to snitch me out. So now that Nivea and I were back reconnected I waited until Caleb stepped out the house to call her. Nivea was now in high school and hated that I was not there to protect her, and trying to keep up with the lies I asked her to tell my friends until I was ready to reveal the truth. She told me how one day Selasi came up to her during the 1st week of school asking if I was coming back. Almost forgetting the pack she and I made, she told her that I decided to stay at the boarding school because I started liking it a lot. She gave her a face of disbelief because she knew me all too well.

"Well if that's the case, why hasn't she called me, or come home to at least visit during school breaks?"

"Omg Tracy, I didn't know what to say and was afraid to spill the tea. So, I just changed the subject by saying that I was going to be late for class."

"I know, Niv, and I don't like how I've put you in the middle. And when I can leave? I promise I'll spend the rest of my life making it up to you."

"You're damn right you are".

We laughed and joked for a few minutes trying to lighten up the mood by talking about typical teenage stuff. I then asked had she seen Demoni around and how mom and dad were doing. My parents were fully aware about as much as Nivea would give them about me running away with my baby. It was hard listening to how it had eaten my dad up to pieces because he had high hopes for me. As for my mom which I already knew, wanted nothing to do with me. If I wanted to be grown and a teen mother so then let me be, and that they weren't going to try and find me. My dad agreed to a certain degree but says he'll never stop loving me and I'd always be his princess.

My sister had to suffer big time because of my mistakes but doesn't blame me for escaping with Sydney, because my mom had no right to try and force to give her up. She also shared with me that she was only allowed to go to and from school. Sleeping over at a friends' house was a no go and she might as well forget about a boyfriend. And the only thing she could do was run track, be black and stay alive. I apologized to her taking away any fun and freedom she might have in the future because of me.

"Don't sweat it, I find plenty of ways to get around those rules placed for me. Trust me, I have fun." When I tried asking her what she meant by that, she said not to worry and when the time was right, she'll tell me all about it. Until then my only job was to be the best mom for Sydney and get my ass home safe.

One day Caleb asked me to sit with him at the kitchen table because he wanted to talk to me about something important. So I picked Sydney up, then sat her down in front of her favorite cartoons so she wouldn't disturb us.

"What's up, babe?"

For almost close to a minute he just sat there looking at me, and then the unexpected happened. He backhanded me across my face so hard, knocking the wind out me causing me to fall to the floor. Never being hit like that ever in my life I began to cry holding my face for dear life. Then I had to peep toward the living room hoping my daughter didn't just witness what had happened.

"What the fuck was that for?"

"Get up and sit back at the table".

Still leaking from the nose and trying not to pass out I found a way to gather myself.

"I had to do that, Tracy, to see if you could handle it."

"Handle what, being abused?"

With his arms crossed he leaned back on the chair with the back two legs planted and began to speak again. After asking me if I knew what he did for a living, he went on to say one of his girls ran away and needed another young pretty worker.

"So, let me get this straight…You're a pimp and you want me to be one of your hoes?"

"Look babe we need this money so I can still keep you and baby girl laced with the finest. Now you already told me you loved me, and the way you be serving this dick I know you're ready for the big leagues."

I wanted to cry again but I also was not up for getting hit again.

Now sitting directly in front of me, he cupped my face with his hands that just hit me and kissed me. I couldn't help but to allow the tears to fall. He told me he was sorry and that he'd never do it again but even as young and naive as I might have been, I wasn't stupid. I nodded and spoke softly,

"Ok."

I asked him why did it have to be me? Why not get another girl?

"Because I trust you, and you'll be perfect for the team."

In addition to being dizzy, my thoughts were all over the place along with now having the biggest headache in the world.

"Mommy crying."

"I'm okay, baby, go sit down and watch Barney."

"Ok, Mommy. Kiss kiss, Daddy."

Caleb picked Sydney up gave her a kiss and together they went outside. I opened the medicine cabinet in the front bathroom, took two Tylenols with a big glass of water and took a nap. I was drained for the 1st time since I gave birth to my daughter except this time the pain wasn't worth it.

Fuck, I should have listened to my mother no matter how much I wanted to keep my baby. But that's what I get for being fast, then thinking I had all the answers just to be worse off than I was really was. No more tears. I thought I was grown so now I must play the role whether I wanted to or not.

My first john was this old nasty ass fucker named Mr. Smitty. He had a thing for young colored girls. He reminded me of Mr. from the Color Purple, just old ugly and nasty. But if he had the money to pay his looks didn't matter. Thankfully the first time he didn't want to do much but talk.

I was way too nervous to do anything so I just followed his lead. Caleb told me that I never had to be nervous because he was always close by. It didn't matter if he was near or far I was not down with this shit but my life depended on it.

"Tell me ya name, pretty girl. I'm Earl but you can call me, Mr. Smitty."

"Nice to meet you, Mr. Smitty."

I really wanted to call him Mr. Shitty breathe because his mouth smelled like he'd been eating ass all day. "Am I your first girl?" He chuckled like old, nasty men do. "My first girl of the day." I looked at him like he was nuts, and repeated,

"First girl of the day?"

"Yes, I can't get enough of the young pussy. I have a high sex drive and my wife is disabled."

"Oh, I see." is all I said.

He began to sit closer to me, finger coiling my hair telling me I smelled good and how he'd marry me if he could. I just smiled and sat motionless, with my stomach in knots trying not to pass out due to his stank ass breath. After we got acquainted a wee bit more he told me to stand up and remove my clothes slowly. I did what I was told because every guy had to rate my performance and I didn't want to get punished for not performing well.

While I was undressing, his eyes were dead on every part of my body while he too took his clothes off. I thought to myself he's a pro pervert for sure. If he could remove his garments without having to look to see what he was doing he's bought way too much pussy. And I also decided on that day I would either need to be high or drunk if I was going to sell my body. Exasperated was the best word to describe the way I felt about what Caleb was making me do.

I just hope that in the future this doesn't affect my willingness to love and being open to try new things.

He traced his old wrinkled fingers across the small of my back, cupped my breast from behind, making moaning noises only a wife could appreciate. He then started to kiss my neck, tickling me a bit as he reached the nap of my curls. I figured at this point it was best for me to stop fighting it and just go with it so it could end fast. Except it didn't, Mr. Smitty was indeed a charmer and unlike young guys he took his time with me, with the intent to make love like artist due with their paintings. He told me to spread my cheeks, and I complied. While I held on to the bed rail he inserted one finger at a time in my opening to get me wet and relaxed. I moaned and moved to the rhythm of his stroke.

"Lay on the bed on your stomach a then arch that fine back for Mr. Smitty."

The next thing I felt was a wide tongue blazing a trail from my spine down to the middle of my pond, where he played in it like a cat going slow at first then fast. Of course, right before I was about to explode, he turned me over kissing me hard while opening my legs with his knees. Not as nervous anymore because we've come too far and I was curious as to how this ride was going to end. I was shocked as how long thick and curvy this old man was, and was worried I wasn't going to be able to take it all in.

"Just relax, baby girl."

I drew in a long breath, then released right before he entered my love below. He pounded me in a slow drag hitting a spot that has never been touched before. I grabbed a hold of his strong back and began to give him what he was giving me.

"Hold on tight."

"Ok", and when I did so he scooped me up and told me to bounce on it.

I did and I rode his ass until my wide legs gave out and he was satisfied. Five hundred dollars later! What I didn't know about the game was that even though I did all the work, I had to pay Caleb a cut which I didn't understand at first.

"Did you get all of the money?" Caleb asked almost ripping the cash out of my hand.

"Yes, I counted it when Mr. Smitty came in the room and once again right before he left."

He nodded at me, motioned for me to get into the car so I could go to the next destination.

"So how many men do I have to sleep with?"

He signaled before getting over in the right lane made the turn and said,

"As many as I tell yo ass today and tomorrow and the next day and the day after that."

He then threatened to slap me if I asked any more fucking questions.

"You need to learn how to stay in a child's place, and as long as you belong to me you will learn how to be the woman I want you to become."

I was slowly learning what kind of monster I got linked up with and if I was going to survive this shit I was going to have to start hardening up quick. Not to mention play the game so I could get out. He was no longer the kind, gentle and respectful man that took me and my daughter in two years ago. So from that moment on I only asked questions I knew wouldn't get my ass kicked, and pretended to be happy for the sake of Sydney and saved the money I made turning tricks.

Caught Up

I had sex with ten men my first day, and wore out isn't even the word to describe how I felt. I couldn't wait to get back to the house so I could soak in a hot bath because my vagina was on fire and swollen beyond recognition. Before I could gather what I needed to bathe Caleb entered the room with an envelope in hand and the biggest grin on his face as if he did me favor.

"Hey, babe."

"Hey", I said barley above a whisper.

"We made a lot of doe today, so after I counted it all and separated it, I put your cut in this envelope."

Remembering not to ask questions I just smiled, took the money and threw it in my backpack.

"Aren't you gonna count it?"

I grabbed my towel, and a blunt I rolled and told him I'd count it later. He must have been cool with that seeing that I worked all got damn day while he played security, because he had nothing to say. He just moved to the side so I could have my space.

I knew once all this was over, I would not be the same person and my feelings about men, trust and love will forever be changed. However, I quickly had to remind myself that I had a daughter to raise and I was going to do my best to hide this other person I was becoming away from her.

Look in the mirror, she has two faces.
One that is familiar and the other unknown
Does she know thyself at all?
What happened to her, they will say.
She had such a bright future, until...
Until she decided to lay with dogs and get fleas.
She had a choice, she should have listened.
Trying to be grown
She should have known there would be trouble.

After I smoked a little bit, reflecting on the day I became desensitized by the minute. I even laughed some as a way to keep from crying which worked at first, but then the tears just feel and kept falling until I had no more energy left in me. I cleaned myself best as I could, dried my body off and put my wet hair into a bun that exposed a bit mark. Before I exited the bathroom, I said a silent prayer for God to help me.

"Hi, mommy, you took so long in the bath."

"Hi, mommy's little princess. How was school today?"

"It was good. Miss Wanda gave us snacks today, and I drew you this."

Trying not to break down at that very moment, I took a deep breath first before I replied.

"Oh my goodness, baby, I love it, now go hang it up on the refrigerator."

I could not believe how much she's grown and talking so well for a two-year-old. She was also getting very tall which she got from both her dad and I. I wish I would have run away with Demoni like he asked I would not be selling pussy right now and living with a man that wasn't Sydney's father. I pray every night that he doesn't do anything to her because if I ever catch him hurting her, I will kill his ass. And that's real!

"Ok", and off she went.

Oh, how I wish I was a kid again and had no worries in the world except for being a good student and pleasing my parents. But those days for me were long over and now I was living a life in the fast lane with the devil himself. After being lethargic from the day I had, all I wanted to do was take a little nap. And that's exactly what I did. It felt so good to be a peace for a while, to be untouched from strangers all over my body. I often asked myself, "I am going to be alive long enough to tell my story?"

"Come and sit on daddy's lap a while." And I did with my legs spread wide like I was giving birth again. He played with my pond like he was plucking a violin, my body moving up and down slow. Then fast. Our hearts were racing for dear life, yet at a pace that allowed us to keep the momentum going. My breast was fondled as he gyrated his number up against my dirty body. "Close your eyes and relax!"

I couldn't believe he had me looking into the mirror while he had his way with me. Not sure what was going to happen next if I closed my eyes. I did it anyways for thrill. Erol pulled my neck back towards him with a fist full of my hair in hand. HE started licking both sides of my neck aggressively. Strangely enough I enjoyed it.

Motherfucker even had the nerve to bite me leaving a small love mark. Except it wasn't love, it was lust. The room was growing hotter and mustier as he then kissed me deeply, taking my breath away. I was playing in a grown woman's game and I had no choice but to comply and make daddy this money. "Oh, shit I'm getting wetter." I can feel him inside, sliding in and out, in and out, in and out. FUCK"!

"Mommy, wake up!"

That was ten years ago since all of this drama began. Who also would have thought I would overcome my obstacles that stood before me? Although I lost custody of my daughter for a while, I was able to get my life back in order. She was also with someone who loved and deserved her more than me, so I was ok with not having her in my life on a daily like before.

While I was in county jail for 6 months all I could think about was my daughter, and what I was going to do with my newfound freedom. During the first few weeks I was scared to death because I was in a place I'd heard so many horrible things about and was surrounded around people who committed crimes worse than me. I thanked God every night that I was caught in Caleb's prostitution ring because I no longer had to endure the abuse from him or sleep with men I didn't know. I felt low and dirty. After I was fingerprinted and booked, I was asked if there was anyone I wanted to call, and I immediately called my dad at his office hoping 1st he was there and willing to take my call.

"Daddy."

"Princess, is that you?"

"Yes, daddy I'm in Folsom County Jail."

"What? Ok, Tracy baby, calm down. We'll get you out as soon as we know the procedures in doing so."

"Okay, daddy, I'm sorry I ran away and I love you."

"We love and miss you, too.” Then all I heard was you have two seconds left on this call and then it disconnected. I was then given a jumper with a long number attached to it and was told to get comfortable because I was going to be in here a while. I thought I was going to lose my mind. I was confined in a small space, the women looked at me like they knew I didn't belong and I just hoped I didn't have to fight any of them. Since I didn't have any reliable friends or family in Sacramento, I hoped that my parents would be willing to pay my bail for me so that I could be released until my court proceedings.

The only person who would get in the way of that was my Queen evil mother, and I was right.

After hearing about Caleb's arrest, I knew it was going to be all bad for me, but all I could do was pray, be patient and ride it out. After being in for a month my parents came to see me, which surprisingly was a great reunion. My mom came in for a hug first with full tears in her eyes, "Tracy, baby, what happened? Why did you run away?"

My dad let her have her moment then he planted as many kisses on me as he could and held my hand the whole entire visit. I told my story of why and how I got to this point and how I just wanted Sydney back. They both smiled as they both told me she was in good hands and how pretty she was. I asked who had her but they wouldn't tell me so I let it be for now, it was my fault anyway right? My parents went on to say they'd do anything to help me get my life back in order by supporting me the best way possible.

My dad found me a great attorney and everything. Once I realized something was off, I asked my Mom where Nivea was and she told me she moved out shortly after graduation and wasn't sure. I felt so bad about that because it's my fault she lost her way and was punished for mistakes I've made. Although we talked off and on, on a regular she never gave me any impression that she had lost her way. I'm guessing she's been fabricating stories but none of that mattered right now. I would handle it once I got out. As I looked back at everything that transpired over the course of four years, I could not believe how I survived somethings but was glad in a sense because it proved I was strong and could overcome anything.

Apparently, Caleb was known for charming young girls breaking them all the way down to turn them into tricks. I also found out that his daughter was a product of prostitution. He met the mother of his daughter Tiffany when she was down and out on her luck with nowhere to go. The other women who testified talked about their stories as well, which were sort of similar and although some were still in the game, others had got themselves together and made a better life. I too was going to find a way to move past this chapter because I was not built for this lifestyle.

Demoni was beyond elated that he was back with his daughter like the day she was born. For days he would just stare at her and watch her every move because he'd missed so much. Then at night he would just cry because he prayed to God and asked him what did he do so bad to deserve this.

I kept playing the many scenarios of how Tracy could keep her away from me then take our baby to live with a complete stranger. I had a few calls over the course of four years from her where it sounded like she wanted to leave a message but didn't or couldn't.

Or, right when I was getting ready to answer it, she would hang up before I had a chance to say hello.

I pushed through my last year of high school alone living with the secret of me being a father all because it's what her family wanted me to do. No one ever seemed to care about how I felt about any of this drama except for her sister Nivea. And for years she kept me in the loop as to how Tracy was doing but only to a certain extent, purposely leaving out where she was and with whom. We even became intimate for a while as a way to cope with the dealings of Tracy running away. Other times it was out of pure revenge for me and when the liquor took over, we indulged in some reckless behavior. It hurt like hell because I was in love with Tracy but she hurt me so bad. I no longer cared about her feelings. She didn't spare me my feelings or did she think about Sydney.

When I got the call from the social worker, I thought it was a joke in that I just knew I had lost my daughter forever. I was told that Tracy and some dude name Caleb Wallace had been arrested leaving Sydney at home alone for days.

She was sleep deprived from crying, and hungry with the exception of the many peanut butter and jelly sandwiches she made herself. But one day a neighbor walked by and noticed something was a wee bit off and made her way in the house. And sure enough my daughter was asleep on the sofa, with her thumb in her mouth and baby doll clutched to her chest.

Right away the police were called but until they arrived, she cleaned her up, fed her then put her on some fresh clothes. I am forever grateful for Brenda Jackson for saving my daughter's life. Apparently, Tracy had been writing in a journal she secretly kept in the room she shared with our daughter that gave police some great tips of how to locate her family.

Since I'm Sydney's father I had all rights to my child. I was so happy I finally got justice because it was Tracy's parents' fault anyway for trying to make her give up our child.

If they weren't so damn worried about keeping up with the Joneses and supporting their daughter she would have never ran away. Then to finally hear the truth how they never wanted me involved made me have ill feeling and resentment towards her family.

Thank God though I was now grown and mature and able to handle the situation like a real man. I allowed them to see their granddaughter because I realized it wasn't her fault her grandparents were ignorant. When we all met up I told the Porter's that I going to fight to have sole custody of Sydney and that they could see her if they liked, however Tracy was not to know that I had her until I was ready.

Per usual her mother wanted to fight but Mr. Porter had his man pants on for once and shut her down, agreeing with me 100%. I was able to support and raise my daughter well due to me being in the NBA and mother who was now retired would care for her while I was on the road.

I must admit I was nervous to take on this new role but ready to finally be in my daughter's life. I was for sure going to hold on tight and never let go. The first year was challenging for sure in that Sydney would cry every night for her mother which was understandable. I was a stranger and her life seemed to have changed almost overnight. She drew close to my mother fast I'm assuming because she was a woman and the only man she knew to be her father was Mr. Wallace. Ole fucking pervert, child molester. How could he think a tenth grader was ready to be in the kind of relationship he made Tracy be in? Then she was a teen mother at that? Just goes to show he had little or no respect for women and to think he also has a daughter. What if it were his child, how would he feel!

After about six months of my life forever changing, the best thing happened. Moms had put Sydney to bed for the night and I was chilling in my bed watching a recap of the game we played against the Lakers. It was about 1:30 am and baby girl came in hair wild, with her baby doll in tow.

"Daddy, can I sleep with you?"

Oh my God did she just say what I think I heard, finally I was daddy!! I was on the verge of tears, but I held it together, "Yes princess you can sleep with daddy every night if you want to."

She gave me a bear hug, a wet kiss then fell asleep on my chest until the sun rose in the morning. Talk about a win-win situation.

Everything Gets Better With Time

The first order of business was completing high school, so that I could then go off to college and be the mother to my daughter the right way. When I got outta jail and was on my ride home all I do was thank God and cry. God had mercy on my soul. I could have really been messed out beyond repair, dead even with no opportunity to live a real decent life.

"Ma, daddy, where is Sydney. I've asked you guys several times where my child was and each time, I got either the run around or the topic would change".

"I understand she has been your life for the past four years but due to the mistakes you made, she is in the care of her father."

Oh my gosh my baby was with her father? I was happy to hear but sad at the same time because I knew I was going to have to fight to get her back. Demoni deserves her just as much as I do, and I was going to do whatever it takes to prove to people I am trustworthy, and responsible. No one is perfect and I need a second chance. In the meantime, I'm going to take the time to get myself together and allow Demoni to be the parent I didn't let him be due to my own selfishness. And of course, my mother had to put her two cents in, and for once I agreed.

"We wanted to take her in once we found out she was safe. But it was our fault in the first place for trying to take her away from you and Demoni for the sake of looking good around town."

Mom and dad told me how people were beginning to talk about how I was missing and how the family was tight lipped. Over time connections were made and our secret was out the bag. At first they were embarrassed, then they felt bad about pushing me to the limit in which I felt I had no other choice but to run away.

"And that poor Demoni was having a real hard time dealing with the fact that he'd lost you and the baby."

Dad drove silently as Mom talked about how the past four years really changed everyone for the better. Well maybe not with Nivea. She felt like she wasn't important and rebelled every step of the way because my parents tried to keep a close grip on her due to what I did. I asked my sister if she was ok, and every time she told me yes it was a lie. I could be mad at her for not being honest but I understand how she felt wanting to be free to be and do whatever and couldn't. Wishing that the situation never happened but was too late to change the series of event.

"Damn guys, I really messed up and I'm so sorry, Mom and Dad, that I caused so much turmoil for everyone."

Then dad cleared his throat and said it was all water under the bridge and that I was forgiven.

"So, young lady, what is your plan now that you're free from that monster?"

I sighed long, and hard to keep the tears at bay because I was just given a whole heap of new information. What I thought I was so sure about I now feel uncertain about.

"Ma, Dad...where is Nivea?" My Mom turned around, placing her hand on my knee, "We don't know, sweetheart. Last thing we heard was that she was staying in Hollywood somewhere."

Hollywood?? What in God's name is in Hollyweird and why was Niv there. Didn't seem like her thing, but one thing was for sure I was going to make it my business to find her if it took my whole life.

One thing for sure, I missed home. I couldn't wait to take a much-needed shower, get into my own bed and close my eyes. Several hours later, with a messed-up bun and droll on my pillow I smelled something amazing! I wasn't sure exactly was it was at first but then something told me to look outside my room window. The backyard was set up like the 4th of July and Dad had on is grill clothes. So clearly, I slept the night away, and it was the next day, which meant time to get my life together and join whatever function my family had going on. Once again, I showered, set my curls with my moose and gel, and brushed my teeth.

It was at that moment I realized I hadn't really looked at myself and in four years I let myself go a bit. I was still pretty and youthful I just looked a bit tired and my eyes had bags under them. Not for long I told myself. I had a few cuts and brushes on my body as well from the abuse but over time those will heal. Right now, it was time to see what today had in store for me. No more living as a victim or punishing myself for my past. Today, I was going to have a positive attitude.

Once I was all dry and partially ready, I went back into my room and found some clothes I was shocked I could still wear. Rushed downstairs to see mom's in the kitchen working on some sides for the meat dad was preparing.

"Oh good morning princess".

I laughed. Mom hadn't called me that since I was 12.

"You mean, afternoon, Mom?" She gave me the biggest hug and kiss and told me to grab a hold of an apron today was a celebration. I wasn't about to argue with a woman who had a knife in her hand.

"Yes, mam."

My dad thought it would be nice to invite friends and family over for some good ole southern cooking and to celebrate my being back home. I wonder who would all be here today? Hopefully my best friends I hadn't spoken to over 4 years and Demoni and our daughter. Dang I miss her so much.

At about two thirty people started to arrive. I was a bit nervous because I hadn't seen anyone in so long. My aunt Monica and uncle Marvin showed up a little after I woke up and we talked, hugged and kissed and even shed a little tear. I'm sure by the end of the day I'm going to be drained just like the first time Caleb put me to work. These emotions however were the good ones and I was all for it. The music was blaring and the heat was beating on my body like the 1st day of summer. Then out of the blue I heard, "Diva"! Without turning my head I knew it was Selasi, and by her side was the prettiest little girl ever!

"Diva," I yelled out. We ran towards one another and locked arm which seemed like forever.

Thank God there were plenty of children around because Selasi's daughter Imani was being ignored by us something crazy.

"To be honest T, I wasn't even gonna come today but your mother explained some things to me and asked me not to hold you totally accountable".

I thanked her from the bottom of my heart for understanding and I promised her that I would give her the full disclosure of how my life spiraled a few times and made it out to share my story. From that day on we've been joined at the hips just like the first day of 1st grade when we met. A few people were missing but I wasn't going to let their absence ruin the day I've had so far.

I couldn't help but think about how rude it would be if Demoni hadn't shown up. Becoming a little overwhelmed I excused myself for a bit and went up to my room to look for a number I had for my sister Nivea. I needed to talk to her right now more than anyone but all I got was a full voicemail. "Fuck." I heard a bunch of people yelling and screaming and instead of panicking I kept my cool, and there he stood. Demoni, point guard for the Clippers Thomas. My heart was beating so fast I wasn't sure if I was dreaming, dead or alive. All I knew was that he was ever more gorgeous in person than on tv. Looks like he got taller as well. My little cousins were all in his face asking for autographs and selfies and he was most happy to do so.

I knew he could feel me watching him but he took his time with each person before saying enough and that he'd get whoever he kissed later. After shaking hands with Dad and kissing Mom, which was weird because as far as I knew they hated him, but things obviously changed.

"Tracy baby, let me look at you."

Not sure to be giddy or serious I only smiled some and then came in for a hug I often dreamed and longed for.

"Demoni, I'm so sorry." He put a finger on my lips requesting me to stop whatever I was about to say. Instead he grabbed my hand and we started to walk out the backyard.

The first five minutes of our walk was in silence, and I was so nervous at first because it's been years of no contact. I wasn't sure what to expect from him, so I just pretended to be okay and go with the flow.

"Tracy, when I heard you were found I was elated. Then got very upset quickly after because if you would have listened and trusted me you and Sydney would have been taken care of."

Not sure if he was finished so I still stayed quiet. After a while he knew where I was and that I was ok because eventually Nivea began to fill him in on everything that was going on with me and claimed I wanted to be in Sacramento. I couldn't help but to chuckle at the last part because that was far from the truth.

Furthermore, after some time Nivea and I stopped talking completely. I figured she was busy with school so I didn't have any resentment towards her. I on the other hand was battling some real shit and was embarrassed to the max about how I was living my life.

"So, take me back four years ago, in the hospital on the day our daughter was born."

He wanted to hear my side because I'm sure my parents filled his head with a bunch of bull and then he naturally made his own assumptions. I stopped in the middle of our stroll and looked him square in the face. I wanted him to see my pain in the rawest form.

I explained to him how my mother made me feel unwanted and the lowest of the low for being a pregnant teen. She was ok with making me give up my rights to be a parent as if she was perfect. What I needed then was support from my parents and I got none. Then to be sent away to hide that I was pregnant, keeping away from him was even worse.

"I thought I knew everything at 16 and the plan I put together was perfect. I was only going to be gone long enough to get my thoughts together and then reunite with you once I turned 18. Except I was tricked and turned out to be one".

I began to sob because I forced myself a long time ago to hide my emotions and toughen up. The line of work I was in was not for the weak.

Demoni cried with me. And we hugged for what seemed to have been for hours. Then like always he gave me the forehead kiss, looked me in the eyes and told me everything was going to be fine and that he was going to help me move past this. Thank God I have great people in my life and that I didn't have to go through this alone. There are women who face challenges alone every day. Some succeed, while other don't. I was going to work extremely hard and one day Syd was going to be proud of me. I just hope she doesn't hate me, and over time she understands what happened and why I felt I had to do what I did.

After our little kumbaya moment we headed back to the house where I'm sure the food was good and ready. And I was beyond hungry. Demoni excitedly talked about how it was love at first site again once he had Sydney. He told me she was a little standoffish at first but receptive of his mother. I'm sure that was because she was a woman and was simply missing me. We'd never been apart before so I can imagine what was going through her little mind.

"I was going to bring her with me today but decided against it until we had our talk first"

"I understand. So how are we going to do the co-parent thing Demoni?"

'We'd have to go back to court because of right now I have custody which I deserve every bit of her".

"I won't argue with that. But I am her mother and been taking care of her since birth".

"Tracy let's not mess this celebration up your parents put together for you. We'll talk about it, let's say tomorrow. We're both emotional right now and I wouldn't want to mess up any chances of us working out an agreement that is suitable for all parties involved".

I wanted to throw a fucking fit. Who does he think he is? He gets a little shine at being a father and all of a sudden, I don't matter!

"You know what, you're right let's go and eat".

I let go of his hand and marched into the house, up the stairs to my room and yelled as loud as I could. After I gathered myself, I counted to ten before exiting the room and joining the rest of my family. I had been selfish enough and today I was going to think about everyone else other than myself for a change.

Before I could make a serious attempt to get my high school diploma, I had to find my sister Nivea and was not about to stop until I did. I asked Demoni and Selasi if they could ask around the city if anyone heard from her, or possible whereabouts.

It was a rough start because most of the people who use to be close to her in school said that she became very withdrawn her last year of high school and didn't hang out with anyone.

While trying to figure out where my sister could be, I got a phone call from Demoni one afternoon.

"Tracy, we need to talk."

Oh boy, this can't be good. "Is Sydney alright?"

"Yes, baby girl is just fine. She's at school right now and she says she can't wait to see you for dinner later".

I waited for him to stop blabbing because I could detect something was wrong.

"While you were in Sacramento your sister and I use to talk often, almost every day during my college days." While he talked and I listened I felt as though I already know where this conversation was going and I needed for him to hurry up.

"Demoni, spit it out!"

"Nivea and I use to fuck each other, and one night we got smashed and didn't use protection. She got pregnant."

"Ok, so you have another child, and it's with my fucking sister? You've got to be kidding me."

No wonder she stopped taking my calls. And all this time I just figured she had a hard time dealing with me being gone and my parents not allowing her to live a normal life because of me.

"So, where the fuck is she, Demoni?"

"Tracy, I know I fucked up and I'm sorry. It didn't happen right away, it just kinda came out of nowhere; but, honest to God, I don't know where she is. Furthermore, she lost the baby".

If there were ever a time I wanted to kill someone it would be after hearing that the father of my child and sister slept together. And she had the nerve to call him ugly, ain't that a bitch! So after I cussed him out, but quickly checked myself because what I did was no better, I then asked him what suggestions he had in helping me find her. According to one of his boys Nivea has been dancing at the Firecracker Strip Club for some time now and we should start there.

There was no way my sister was a stripper. She doesn't like attention like that. Before we got off the phone, I told Demoni that after dinner with baby girl, we'd drop her off and head to Irvine to the club, to see if Nivea was there or if anyone knew who she was. Seeing Syd and Demoni together made me a little jealous but happy all at the same time.

Looking at them at the same time was crazy, Demoni stopped in his tracks pointed in my direction for Sydney to look and she took off like a rocket. "Mommy, mommy."

We hugged and kissed for almost ten minutes. She asked me why I left her and when was I coming to daddies to get her. I wasn't sure what to say because Demoni and I were still trying to figure it all out plus I didn't want to ruin the night.

"Are you hungry, baby?"

"Oh my goodness Mommy I am starving. School was long today, and daddy said I had to wait until I got my surprise first".

"He did. And what was the surprise baby?"

"You, mommy duh"! The whole time we talked Demoni just sat there and listened observing our interaction.

"Daddy, isn't Mommy pretty?"

"She sure is princess just like you." He gave me a wink like back in the day and then he called over the waiter so we could order our food.

We shared more stories of the day and small talk and everything and I was super hyped about finishing school.

"Whatever you need, I'll be right here. Right, Sydney?"

With macaroni all over her little mouth and hands she managed to give a thumbs up and a high five to her dad before sipping on her apple juice. So, this is what it's like to have both my loves together in one room. As much as I wanted Demoni too much time has passed and I wanted to focus on me right now.

I followed Demoni and Sydney to the house so we could bath and read a bedtime story before our search for Nivea. We were greeted by Ms. Beverly, who my daughter has become very fond over in such a short time. What I wasn't expecting was for her to embrace me like she did. For the first time in a while I was happy.

"Tracy baby let me look at cha. You look the same just older. I'm so glad that you're okay and that I finally get to spend time with this beauty you and my son made".

We talked a little more, hugged and kissed again and then she retired up to her room for the night as me and Demoni headed out on our mission.

On our drive to Irvine Demoni and I talked about co- parenting Sydney and I listened to everything he said before I interjected.

"After seeing you and Syd go back and forth tonight, I can't keep her from you. But what I will say is that I want her with you as long as you'll allow." I nodded in agreement. "I see how much she adores you and because you have rights that I took away from you, I'll do whatever you want".

During basketball season she'd be with me and I'd share her with grandma Beverly and then during off seasons Demoni would have her. On family nights we'd all get together and do things as one.

Before I knew it, we were at Firecracker and it was time to see why Nivea just vanished. I prayed all the way there that she would be there and receive me with open arms. We paid to get in and because Demoni was a celebrity we got a VIP section and the DJ had announced that he was in the building. Then out of the blue all the girls came flocking to our table.

"Damn, have you been here before"?

"Not in a while".

I wanted to go off, but I didn't because we were in public, and anytime I sassed with Caleb I was hit. Not sure if Demoni was capable of being violent, but I didn't want to find out either.

"Aww shit", one of the dancers said from the backroom to Nivea. Did you hear who they said was in the building bitch?"

Before she answered Tasha, she thought to herself *I know I didn't just* hear *what I did. Why was he here*"? *I knew I shouldn't have come tonight. Fuck*!! Nivea hadn't seen or heard from Demoni since losing the baby. But I guess that was her fault for sleeping with her sister's baby daddy huh? She scanned the room from behind the DJ booth to see if it was real but all she could see was ass and titties at a table which let her know exactly where Demoni was seated.

As I sashayed over I noticed another person. A woman. Oh really?!!! Then I took a step back and blinked a few times because who I saw was a girl who looked just like me. Tracy? Nah couldn't be, she was in the Bay and wanted nothing to do with us anymore. Just when I was about to step up to her Tracy looked her dead in the face.

"Nivea."

My first thought was to run out of shame, but I missed my sister so much I ran toward her.

"Tracy!".

I guess I'm glad I did come in after all. God must have known the reason and I thank him for bringing her back to me. I headed back to the dressing room, changed my clothed and bounced. I drove back with Demoni and Tracy, to where I didn't know at first and didn't care.

As Demoni drove us we sat in the back of the SUV talking a mile a minute as if we didn't have the rest of our lives to catch up. But 4 1/2 years was too long. We came to a stop at a house that looked like a castle which only meant we were at Demoni's. After entering, Demoni said good night and let us stay in one of the unused rooms. Tracy and I talked until we were blue in the face, we cried and then fell asleep with our hands touching.

Then out of nowhere someone jumped on the damn bed scaring the shit out of both of us. Demoni just stood there looking, while this little person jumped on us. "Mommy, you came back".

"Yes, baby, Mommy came back, and I'm never going anywhere, okay".

"OK!"

"Say hello to Aunty Nivea".

"Good morning, Aunty Nivea. Can I have a hug too"?

"Yes, maaaam. I haven't seen you since the day you were born".

"You met me before, Aunty Nivea?" the two of them completely ignored Demoni. We joined hands and walked about the house.

Emotional and overwhelmed as I was, I was on cloud nine and I wasn't coming down.

"Did you sleep well, Tee?" Demoni asked.

"Yes, I did, and what is that smell?"

His mother was down stairs making breakfast. There were omelets, bacon, toast, waffles, hash browns, a bowl of fruit, coffee, and orange juice.

"Good morning, Nana, this is Aunty Nivea".

Ms. Beverly stopped what she was doing, gave everyone a hug followed by good morning and continued doing her thing that was clearly a typical routine. Later that day my parents joined us for dinner, with no idea as to why, since it wasn't anyone's birthday or holiday. But it was indeed a celebration. Nivea was back!!

The New Chapter

Where there is a party celebrate,
and dance like no one is watching.

A few weeks later I started back going to school to complete my GED, then college next. I was on a roll and nothing was going to stop me now, or ever again the old Tracy Marie Porter was back. While working on getting me together my support system was strong as ever cheering me on along the way. I failed once already and I was not going to do anything in the mean time to let them down and shame them again. Feeling like a big girl now at 22 I decided I was going to rent me a little apartment to have my space and to have a place that my daughter could call her own when she came to stay with me.

Since I didn't have any credit or prior rental history, Demoni offered to lease one for me in his name. Of course, he wanted to go all out, and I let him because it was not just for me. Instead of an apartment I ended up with a cute little house in Huntington Beach by the water that I absolutely love. The street was serene like I like, away from the chaos of the city which will allow me to focus of school and my daughter.

Due to me out growing my room and everything in it at my parents, I was going to have to start from the bottom. I was fine with that since I loved to shop anyways. Mom has a good eye for decorations so I took her up on the offer to help me find everything I was going to need for the house.

Sydney was also excited to have her say on how her room would look since the one at her dad's house was already laid before she arrived.

The week that I moved into the house I also completed my GED and of course anytime an achievement occurred it caused for a celebration. My sister came around more which was great because I was going to need all my day ones, Selasi and Nikki too. As a matter of fact, every month we promised to spend a day together doing something different every time.

Usually on Wednesday night at the Lava Lounge the girls and I would meet us for happy hour to catch up and have some drinks while the music played in the background.

My sister had opened up more disclosing more with me about how traumatic my running away was for her and how for a while she resented me which led her to fall back some. I understood her feelings and wasn't upset at all. I still felt some type of way about her and Demoni but chose to keep my mouth closed about it until she was ready to talk to me about it. I thought it was kind of funny how she always mentioned how good Demoni and I looked together and how we should give it another try as if I didn't know they fucked around.

"Maybe one day when the time is right. Right now, I'm just glad he forgave me and that Sydney and I have him in our lives".

"I guess you're right, sis. He grew up quite nicely".

"Yeah, I know, for an ugly nigga, huh?" We laughed and joked about how she used to talk about him so badly and I didn't care if he wasn't attractive. He was all mine and I was fine with that. I never had to worry about girls trying to holla at him while we dated, plus he only had eyes for me.

Due to me not finishing school the traditional way and not taking the SAT's like most of my classmates, I had to provide the college I was applying to the only high school credits I did have, take assessments and all that jazz before I could get in. Thank God my mom was an educator and could get around loopholes most people don't know about. Not to mention she now taught English Lit at UCLA, so tuition was free (not that money was an issue); but, thank God I didn't have to worry about it. I was a nervous wreck waiting by the mailbox every day for my acceptance letter; so, I kept myself busy.

I began painting the rooms in the house, rearranging furniture where I wanted them to go and planning my housewarming party that I wanted to share with the closest people to me. It was also my weekend with baby girl and I had lots of fun things planned. For starters I took her shopping at her favorite clothing store, which was Old Navy. Then we went to the Disney Store, Toys R Us and then for a quick bite to eat. Afterwards she was food wasted and she fell asleep like always. Later on, we both went to the nail shop for mani and pedis where we met up with Selasi and her daughter Imani who was just two years older than Sydney. Then to end the perfect night we grabbed some movies and snacks, went back to the house and had our 1st real slumber party.

My heart began to race because I went all day not thinking about the mail, and before I retired for the night something said go check the mail Tee. So I did, and guess what was in there finally?

I went to my room, closed the door and tore open the letter from UCLA administration department. I read it silently, then out loud to make sure it was real, then I screamed without waking up the girls. My eyes suddenly were filled with tears of joy and I couldn't contain my excitement that I had to call the one person who hasn't let me down so far.

"Demoni, are you sleep?"

"You know I'm a night owl. How was the girls' day?"

"Great, Sydney and Imani fell asleep watching a movie in the living room".

"Oh ok, babe, what's up?" Hardly able to sit still I walked around the house as we talked, and I told him that I got into UCLA. He congratulated me and said that he wanted to do something special for me and that he would let me know once he had all the plans laid out. Since he had an away game it would have to be when he returned to LA. I was in no hurry. We talked a little while more, then said good night. I locked all the doors in the house and checked the windows for good measure and went to bed.

Two weeks later we met up for dinner to celebrate another milestone. Since it was a date I was told to get dolled up for the special occasion. I wasn't sure what to expect but to be on the safe side after buying a cute dress and getting my hair and nails done, I waxed my kitty and shaved my legs. And considering how long it's been since I've been on a horse, I figured I'd be ready to put on my cowgirl hat and ride'em!

Demoni picked me up like a real gentleman in a limo, where we dined at Ruth Chris for dinner. Afterwards he took me to this little jazz spot, where he hoped crazed fans or paparazzi weren't going to be following us.

Half way through our date I had decided I was going to give him some because he was playing all his cards right, collecting all of brownie points. After all he was my first love, and somethings just don't change.

"So tell me about your experience in Sacramento that's if you're ready to share."

I gave him play by play of the last four years with Caleb, the people I met while there, how I was tricked into being a trick all the while keeping my sanity.

"No wonder you weren't very receptive of me touching you".

"You picked up on that?"

"I think I know you pretty well Tracy even if we been apart for a while".

"I thought I was playing if off pretty well. Maybe what has happened to me has affected me beyond repair. Wow, I hadn't even noticed my behavior. By the way when did you get so smart?"

"Haha. You got jokes, huh?! I've seen some things and in case you forgot, I did go to college."

Just when I was about to say something else, he reached across the table touching me right above my mouth.

"You also have a scar just above your lip that wasn't there before. Did he do that to you?"

As much as I wanted to lie and blame it on my accident-prone self, I know I could trust Demoni in telling him the truth. I tried to not think about the things I went through with Caleb. It took everything in me not to get angry all over again and cry. "Yes".

"I'm sorry if my asking was inappropriate."

I touched his hand to reassure him that I was ok and that it wasn't his fault some men couldn't keep their hands to themselves. Although a victim I tried to not play like one for the sake of my daughter. I also know to some degree it's my fault because I allowed it to happen and if I had only left after the first time I wouldn't be left with emotional scars.

I took a long breath and began to spill some tea. Demoni could tell I was getting ready to speak so he put his fork down for a minute to listen.

"At first things seemed really normal between Caleb and I, as if we were a real family and he treated Sydney like she was his own".

I went on to say that due to our age difference there was no way he'd be interested in me. I was only a child so there was nothing to worry about or fear. Clearly that was a lie, and he didn't care that he was 11 years older than me. From what I hear his baby mama too was young when he met her and turned her out.

It was after the first year that our relationship really changed. I was his girlfriend. He was still sweet though, giving me and Syd what we needed and wanted and I didn't have to ask for anything.

What I didn't like was how much schooling I missed and how he felt that because we had now become a family that my parents, sister and you no longer mattered and after a while I begin to believe that as well. He would often tell me to forget about home, because I belonged to him now. Sydney was getting bigger and becoming more and more attached to him by the day and called him daddy.

I didn't fight him on that because he was providing for her like so and he played the role so well. I even met his daughter a few times, but the baby mama was never allowed in the house. Now that I think about it, I feel like he set it up that way out of fear that Kesha would spill the beans on his true intentions.

Tonight, was supposed to be a celebration of me getting into college, but like life things don't always go as planned. Nevertheless, I was actually enjoying my night. After we finished our small talk we sat quietly for a while listening to the band perform a song that seemed to sound so familiar to what I went through with Caleb. The blues has a way of doing that to people, which is why I love it so much. I can remember a night when he came home drunk and I was already sleep. He pulled the covers off of me kissing me all so aggressively and as I started to tell him to stop and to wait until the morning for us to have sex. He slapped my face, telling me to shut the fuck up and turn over like a good hoe is supposed to do.

Knowing what he was capable of and didn't want to be hurt any worse, I complied. He took me from the back, raw for the first time after I told him I wasn't down with that nasty shit. He then spit in between the crap of my ass, fingering me a little before he entered my hole. I thought I was going to die or throw up. It was more than just an unexpected surprise since I had already told him I was not a fan of anal sex and I wanted him to stop.

Afraid to say so, I just silently cried as he pounded inside of me until he couldn't get enough. He immediately passed out after, and I found enough strength to get out the bed and drew me a hot bath, sat in it for an hour and wept myself silly.

Caleb woke up the next morning all calm and shit, whistling even. "Good morning, bae".

"Good morning, Caleb".

"Damn! What happened to your face, and why you moving so slow?"

Was he serious right now? Had he been so drunk that he didn't even remember raping me last night, his own fucking girlfriend? I had to be careful about how I responded because I was way too cute to be his punching bag. And, of course, the last thing I wanted was for my daughter to freak out.

"You don't remember?"

"Naw, that's why I'm asking you."

I sighed and took a breath before answering. "Things got a bit out of hand last night when you came home drunk demanding sex".

"We had sex? Hmm, I don't remember. Damn that dark liquor ain't no joke."

I couldn't believe he really had no clue and I wonder how many other women and young girls had he done this to.

"Well, did we have fun at least?"

"Yes", was all I said.

All of a sudden, the built-up curiosity of having sex with Demoni again was no longer on my mind. I felt dirty all over again. I did however want to go home and have him cuddle with me. I told Demoni I was no longer in a good mood and wanted to go home.

I asked him if he would just lay with me until I feel asleep, he agreed and we left the club going back to my house.

The ride home was quiet, and not because Demoni had did anything wrong. All the talk about Sacramento and Caleb brewed up some things I wanted to keep buried and forgotten forever. I wanted to let Demoni know just how special tonight had been but not until my mind was clear.

"Make yourself comfortable while I go change."

I peeled my clothes off, took me a hot steamy shower with hopes all the memories of Caleb's abuse and being a prostitute would be washed away forever. After about twenty minutes I lathered up with my favorite vanilla body butter and a cute little teddy I purchased a few months back. When I re-enter my living room the mood had been set, with soft music playing, candles lit and two glasses of wine filled to the rim.

"Wow, babe, just when I thought tonight had gone sour, you took it up another notch."

Standing right in front of each other he said, "I felt so bad about the last thing we talked about at the jazz club that I felt I had to apologize."

I looked Demoni straight in the eyes and grabbed his hands assuring him that it was ok, and that the change of pace was nice for a change. He then took my hands, kissed them both and invited me in with a full-on kiss that caused an electrifying entanglement with our tongues. I stopped abruptly because I didn't want the night to end just yet.

"Why did you stop?"

"Today has been amazing and I wanted to tell you that before I forgot and I figured we could talk a little bit more first before we got lost in paradise".

It was then I noticed he too was ready for bed with some silk pajamas on. "I see that you come ready!"

"It's not like that, I hadn't unpacked my trunk and once you told me to make myself at home, I remembered I had extra clothes. So while you were showering, I showered in the guest bathroom and slipped into this."

As he twirled around showing off his body, I couldn't help but laugh. Almost out of the blue be blurted out, "You know I still love you right?"

OMG my heart was beating so fast. Was he for real or was the mood he'd set part of a game men love to play? Whatever it was, I was all for it.

"I love you too, Demoni. I never stopped." He scooped me up so quick.

"Where is the bedroom, babe?" Lost in his eyes and fixated on his lips, I managed to point him in the right direction. He laid me on the bed, left for a few seconds and returned with our drinks and candles he lit.

"When did you get romantic?"

"I learned a couple of tricks".

He kissed, licked and sucked on my bottom lip like it was a piece of fruit. My mouth was throbbing for more and whatever he gave me that night I threw right back at him. I swear the love me made was against the law and Demoni was putting on a show starting with him re-introducing himself with his beautiful bronze body and a third leg I don't quite remember looking so grown. I took several sips of my wine to prep myself for this ride, and I was going to need Jesus to give me strength to get up in the morning. Now that we were both nude in the dark a few flickers of the candles danced around dangerously. The passion grew deeper with every touch, and with every kiss.

My heart was pounding so fast I thought I was going to faint from not being able to contain my excitement and the adrenaline rush I was experiencing by just being near him. I closed my eyes as he took his tongue and ran it all through my temple starting from my mouth on down to my neck. By the time he reached my breast I thought I was going to start a flood in my room. I held on to him for dear life, allowing him to take over my body and soul.

He stopped, told me to turn around. He then kissed my back, my black bottom, and slowly spread my legs apart. And like a gynecologist he probed my valley with every finger on his hand, then feeding me what was left over.

"Turn over and keep your legs open."

"Yes, yes! Anything you want daddy."

Without skipping a beat, he slid a condom on, and entered my body slowly whispering God knows what, in my ear. All I know was that it felt good to be in his arms again. He then picked me up while still inside and bounced me up and down while he stood up.

I had one arm holding him while the other was suspended in the air like I was riding a horse. I was making all sorts of noises I'm sure my nosey ass neighbors on each side could hear but I didn't care.

"Oh shit, fuck. Yes. Give it to me daddy".

With every demand he pumped harder and faster like a wild animal who hasn't been outside for days. As the ride began to slow down, we collapsed, hot and wet on the sheets, the fire still dancing right along with us.

"Damn, baby, you sure did put it on a nigga."

"Well, recharge your battery, baby, because it's not over yet."

"That's what I hoped you say." He planted a few after sex kisses on me and fell asleep to Tony Toni Tone. "Lay your head on my pillow, and just relax, relax."

Thank God my parents agreed to babysit Sydney for the weekend because as soon as Demoni recharged he went back to getting my motor hot. We went for two more runs until our batteries blew out.

By the time we finished it was twelve noon and since we missed breakfast we decided to shower, dress and go for some food. I felt like a high school girl all over again, beaming with happiness, because I was with the finest boy on campus, except this time he was a man.

We drove to the Marietta Diner, where the wait time was 20 minutes or more. I didn't mind because I was with my love, and I felt like a new woman.

While we waited to be seated, we made small talk, held each other's hands like we used to do, and every now and then we gave one another pecks. Other people were looking at us, but not because of the PDA. It was because of Demoni's celebrity status. He even agreed to take a few selfies with fans and signed some autographs.

I wonder if this type of attention ever got annoying or was he cool with it due to an understanding that this came with the territory. There were even a few thots trying to get his attention for other reasons, not giving a damn that I was sitting next to him. I know they could clearly see that I was not a friend or sister, based on the affection we were showing each other.

I was surprised that he never paid them any mind. Maybe he wasn't like most men in the world (he was three years older than me), or he could have been fronting because he was with me. Whatever the reason, I wasn't pressed. We weren't together and after today I didn't expect us to keep it going. We had two different lives and a promise is a promise.

Demoni and I hung out a few more times and each time it was the same, which meant I was losing control and now the dreadful talk would have to happen.

"Babe, the day you stepped into my parent's backyard, I just knew it was going to be something. What I wasn't expecting was to fall for you all over again."

Wanting to make sure I said everything I needed to and keeping my feelings in check at the same time, I sighed.

"But", Demoni said.

"But, school starts in a week and I need to be completely focused. I promised after the Caleb situation I would solely focus on me for a while and hold off on dating."

"But, we both know I'm nothing like Caleb. I'm D-Nice." He laughed hoping that would change something, and although it was tempting, his career was thriving and to get on his level I couldn't risk any distractions.

"I'm serious babe, I never thought we'd ever link back up and I'll admit the love is still here - a lot stronger, but for once I need to do what's best for me."

He looked like his feelings were hurt, but if he truly loved me he'd understand.

"So, that means no more sex, kisses, late night snuggles?"

"Yes! As much as I would love to keep it going, sex complicates things and the way you put me in your love trance, it's for the best."

He pulled me close as if I said I was going to die in the next 24 hours, told me no one compared to me and he would wait forever if he had to for me to give him the green light. Damn, why does this love thang have to be so hard. Ugh.

"Fine, well since I'm here now, can I get some more of that thing I like one more time?" I kissed his big ole plump lips and got the party started for good old-time sakes.

Basketball season was starting soon and so was school, therefore both of us would be too busy to entertain one another. Plus, I'm sure he had some boo thangs set up in each city he frequented.

My new boo(s) would be my books, exams, our daughter and maybe a hobby to create balance.

I couldn't believe the first four years of college flew by and now I was conquering my first semester as a grad student. Not without its challenges, but hey, that's life. The girls accused me of being too good to hang out, when the truth of the matter was, between classes, papers and being a mom, I was exhausted.

Hell, I hadn't even been to the gym since I decided to join, nor have I gotten a pedicure done in months and forget about my hair. Good appearances in California was a must; but, when you have goals and a deadline to meet, trying to be cute after a while becomes a thing of the past. I couldn't wait until winter break so I could kick my feet up for a few weeks, catch up with my girls, get a home cooked meal from Mom and Dad's house, and have a little fun with my princess who's growing every single day.

I didn't see or hear from Demoni unless it was to check on Sydney and when he or Ms. Beverly's was picking her up. I can't lie, though. I did miss the dick though. I made a few attempts to get to know a few guys while on campus or while riding around the city; but, I ended up empty handed. Out of the blue and not trying hard, I met this dude one day trying to rush out of the bank. His name was Dante.

Dante used to love me so good. Brotha had me addicted like a crackhead or like ya grandmother who needs a pack of cigarettes every two days. He was into any and everything that had to do with sex and the things I vowed to never do again, I did with Dante. We met right before the winter break, and talked on the phone for a while before linking up. I wanted to feel him out some.

Rushing out of the house per usual in taking Sydney's to her dads house I remembered I had to run into the bank to deposit some of the money working for Caleb. I know I was pushing it but I had put it off long enough. To make matters worse the Clinic had a no late policy and I've been waiting in line for over twenty minutes in which should have only taken a few minutes to do. The ATM machines were down and everybody and their mama seemed to be in line.

The bank didn't have enough tellers so everyone was wiggling and sighing and blowing hot air as a sign of their frustrations, including myself. So anyways, as soon as I took care of my business, I dashed out of Chase almost knocking this dude out trying to get out the door. My purse slid off my shoulders and my keys dropped from the impact I can best explain the impact was like being hit by a linebacker with no helmet.

"Damn, girl, don't hurt yourself, you ok?"

Barely catching my breath, I managed to say, "yes," while picking up my keys at the same time.

"I'm so sorry. I'm late and need to get to my destination fast".

"I understand. Where you going, beautiful?"

I chuckled at his choice of words because I felt as though he was using a mac daddy line. I had my hair in a ponytail and I had on black slacks and white collared shirt with no makeup and no jewelry.

"Umm...to school."

He asked me what school I attended and told me he too went to UCLA. While listening to him talk I wondered how come I didn't bump into him sooner. Suddenly forgetting the time for reals, almost at the same time, we asked each other for the digits so we could continue our conversation at a later date. Once in my car I made a serious dash to the freeway. While driving and bumping to some old ass India Arie, I realized I didn't tell the guy my name and wasn't sure if he gave me his either. If he called or texted, I would find out then.

Thank God I was on time!! The last thing I wanted to hear was Ms. Erica's mouth about how unprofessional it was for me to be late for work, blah blah blah.

"Girl, relax."

Two days later I received a text saying, "Good evening, Beautiful. It was nice running into you the other day. I hope I didn't hurt you. You were in such a hurry I never did get your name, mine is Dante. Hope to hear from you soon."

Just the message alone almost made me wet but I only had one day until finals so I had to remain focused. I sent him a quick reply that included my name and that we should get together soon. He texted back "Dido, have a great night." Thank goodness I was getting my hair done because I looked a hot mess. My best friend is a hairstylist. I didn't have to make an appointment to get my hair done no matter how booked she was.

"Well, well, look who the cat drug in."

"Don't start, Selasi. You know I've been all work and no play."

We both laughed and exchanged quick hugs because she had a client under the dryer at the moment and was about to start with another.

"Give me about an hour to finish Pam and start on Nikki and I'll squeeze you in. You can then fill me in and we can go for drinks afterwards. That's if you're not too busy?"

"Oh, shut up, heffa. You know I just finished finals today and have a two- week break. We have lots to catch each other up on."

"Yeah, yeah...well sit back, relax and I'll be right with you."

I Present To You, Dr. Tracy Nicole Porter

A month before graduation I almost had a meltdown. I was overthinking things and was extremely nervous to be a part to the real world. I was not going to be working at a job like some people which there is nothing wrong with that might I add. But I was going to be a career woman. I had a name in the community that people already knew so I couldn't let my myself or parents down. Image was everything in the Porter family. My sister Nivea really came through when I needed her during stressful and trying times. Helping me out with Sydney when I couldn't due to deadlines and such. I'm forever grateful to have her back in my life and seeing that her own life has changed drastically for the better.

I couldn't wait until graduation because this time I was walking across the stage for the second time and everyone who meant anything to me was going to be at USC cheering me on. Mom and dad bragged about me every chance they got especially my dad. And like daddy promised if I delivered, my reward would be my very own office where I planned to service the great people of Los Angeles.

Just several months after I graduated daddy and I had went shopping all over the city and then some trying to find the perfect location and for my office. In addition to that I had to hire a receptionist, buy the furniture and decor and although it took time to do, I had fun bonding with dad.

With all that I had been through I was glad the hard part was over. Being a college student and a parent wasn't always easy, for those who can relate you know the struggle is all too real.

I picked a cozy little number on Wilshire and Grand to open up shop, in the heart of Los Angeles. After doing about a dozen of interviews I picked a very bright college student by the name of Gina Langford. She was driven, well- groomed and seemed to understand exactly what I needed. The last thing I had to do before having an open house was to have some pictures taken. Gina's first task was to find me some fly yet professional outfits for my photoshoot, plus look for a photographer.

Once photos were selected and printed, Gina and I went around with my business cards to give out to colleges, hospitals, libraries, coffee shops and so on.

This was the perfect time to get to know Gina and ask her questions about who she really was as a person. I wanted to form the kind of business environment that was like family and since Gina's going to work super close to me, I wanted to build a foundation of trust and comfortability on both ends. What I learned was that she grew up in a small city in Minnesota, and that it had always been her dream to move to a big city. Since California has great weather and beaches, she took a leap of faith and moved after high school. She enrolled in Cal State Dominguez Hills as an English major but soon figured out her true passion was for helping people.

During her interview I asked her why she wanted to be a receptionist if she was going to school to be a psychologist she said, "If I want to know about the industry that I'm interested in the best way is to get my foot in the door and move my way up".

I was impressed by her answer but what I wasn't sure about is why she would work for a newbie instead of a seasoned therapist. She went on to say that I wasn't set in my ways. I was still passionate and driven, willing to help a college student like herself (since it hadn't been that long that I myself was a college student). It was clear she had done her homework.

We had a few more heart-to-heart moments and before she left my office, I knew she was the right one for me. No more interviews were needed. I had my dad's receptionist, Dolly, come and train Gina for me and bring a few security guys on board to make sure the people and building was going to be safe at all times.

Everything was pretty much set for the opening of my business. I was both nervous and happy with the new chapter I was starting in my life. Mom and dad did one last walk with me, blessing the building as we walked through. Nivea took care of the catering team for me, and of course my girl, Selasi, made sure my hair was laid to the side.

All I needed was the people to flow in like Black Friday; but, I knew it would take some time. I had to trust God and be patient, and the world would be mine (and in the palm of my hands). I invited everyone I could think of and asked them each to bring along a guest. Pictures were taken that night, people were enjoying the music, food and all the networking that was taking place.

Not only was I smiling on the outside, I felt all warm and fuzzy on the inside, as well. As the crowd was mellowing out and I was just about ready to close shop, I heard, "Hey, Beautiful."

"Oh my God, Demoni! How did you know about the party?"

"Well, for starters our daughter told me."

"Hi, daddy!"

"Hey, princess. Did you miss me?"

"Of course, dad." As I watched the two of them bond, I couldn't help but get a little misty because God couldn't have chosen a better man for me to make a mistake with.

"Since I came in town earlier than expected, I figured I could finally go pick up my dry cleaning, and what do you know? I picked up your business card and flyer while there, and knew I had to come. Then as I was driving up on Rodeo Drive on the way to a meeting, I saw your poster, which was another sign that I should come."

My mind was racing a mile a minute. Damn, why did he look so good?

"Well, thank you for coming out and always supporting everything I do."

"And no I was not late either. I've been here for over an hour watching you do your thang. Plus, your dad and I were politicking about sports per usual and before I could get to your mom dukes stopped me for a brief moment. So, I figured I'd wait until the crowd panned out some."

I grabbed his neck so tight and planted the biggest kiss on him ever.

"I missed you so much."

"I guess I should do more pop ups like this to get this kinda love, huh?"

We talked a little bit more until everyone was gone out the building. I waited for my security guide, Monty, to secure the place. Demoni walked me to my car, saying he was going to come over – that is, if I was okay with it. I gave him that look, started my engine and he followed behind me. I was driving so fast, as it's been over two years since Demoni and I last made love and roughly six months since the Derek situation; so, a girl's kitty was purring like crazy.

I got a text from Selasi, saying, "I saw ya man, T. You two need to stop playing and just get back together."

Not able to respond, due to me driving; but, I was able to read it. I just laughed and made a mental note to call her back the next day. Thank God I keep wine and such on stash because I felt like being drunk in love for old time's sake. I hadn't even closed the door to my house good and I was already barking orders. "Take your clothes off."

Without a word Demoni's shirt was off within seconds and shoes were kicked to the side. I headed to the pantry, popped open the cork to some Sweet Red and threw my head back as I took a sip.

"Oh, you're not going to be a lady tonight, huh?"

"Stop talking."

Before I could say another word, Demoni had me up against the wall with my legs spread eagle kissing me from my lips down to my ears and neck, until he reached the mountaintop of kitty land. Just before I was about to erupt, he stopped and I watched to see what else he had up his sleeve. He took out the chocolate whipped cream, strawberries I forgot I had and a bowl of ice. I headed to my room, put on some pandora and removed the top layer of my covers so that it wouldn't get messy.

Demoni told me to hold a strawberry in my mouth as he squirted the whip cream in his and then our lips met. I wanted to explode right there but I didn't want to rush the flow and we had all night. I hated when he teased me but I also knew he was trying to control his climax because he didn't want to look like a chump and cum too fast. This also was a clear indication to me that it had been a long time since he had him some.

I took a cube of ice, placed it on my tongue then slide his hot pocket inside, making him quiver and his toes pop. I had control again and right where I wanted him. I ate some strawberries off his chest along with some whip cream and when I knew he was good and ready I slid on top and rode him slow, then fast then slow again. In turn he flipped me over almost knocking the wind out of me but I quickly grabbed a whole of my bed frame to keep from falling off the ride.

We were both moaning, cooing and making grunting noises to the point I thought the neighbors were going to call 5-0. We went all night and suddenly I needed a cigar, and I don't even smoke.

Just when everything was going perfect, I heard, "I love you, Tracy."

"What the fuck?" I said to myself, and caught up in the moment I whispered that I loved him back, which I did kinda sorta?!! I just didn't know if it was enough to start over just yet. I was not about to spoil a perfect evening, so I just lived in the right now and figured I'd worry about tomorrow later. We spooned, talked and kissed the rest of the night until we fell asleep. We must have both been super tired because we stayed in the bed til almost noon. I woke up to the sounds of Demoni's stomach making noises.

He kissed me with all my stank breath and asked me to shower with him. I know what that means and I was all for it. Thank God I had good hair and didn't mind getting it wet. He lathered me up first massaging my breast and shoulders before moving down to my butt. After he covered my legs he took his thumb and index figure that had soap on it and rubbed my mound until I could no longer stand it. Just when I thought he was done, he told me lift my leg up while he entered my hot spot one finger at a time. As much sex as we had the night before I was sure I had enough but every time I'm with him, my batteries recharge without hesitation.

Since it was no longer breakfast and being beyond hungry after all the good loving we made, we decided to leave the house. We went to Roscoe's Chicken and Waffles off of Pico and La Brea. It was crowded as usual, but I didn't care. I was ready to eat and because I was with a star, it didn't take long for us to be seated. People obviously recognized Demoni and began waving, taking pictures and a few people asked for autographs, which he never refuses. I loved him for that, never telling his fans no.

"I'm sorry, babe," he always says, when this happens.

"It's okay, babe. I'm used to it by now, plus I, too, am your number one fan."

I whispered some other things in his ear that I didn't want anyone hearing. It was my petty way of letting the women who were breaking their neck to flirt with him know that he was mine, even if it was only temporary.

Our server came over to our table to ask if we were ready to order. Per usual I got the #9 which name has been changed to the Obama Special. It came with three wings, waffles, potato salad or fries. Demoni ordered The Oscar that came with chicken wings, grits, two large eggs and fluffy biscuits. I always enjoy my time with Demoni, as he has me laughing all the time, on cloud nine and like I'm the only woman in the world.

So what's the matter, you say? I'm finally getting used to my independence and living life on my own terms. Pardon me for being a tad bit selfish but the real Tracy has finally arrived, and it was gonna have to be business before pleasure for a while. Maybe if I hadn't gotten pregnant, ran away, and gotten turned out I wouldn't be afraid to ride the wave. Most women would kill be to be with a man like Demoni, but I'll always have him because of how we're connected.

I guess you can say I'm still a work in progress.

"Tracy, I noticed that after I told you that I loved you last night you didn't respond. Instead you opted for bedroom eyes and a deep kiss."

Damn man, I had hoped he had long forgot about that part and not bring it up. Now I had to face the music.

"Demoni, I have no doubt that you love me, and although the feelings are the same, I'm just in a different place in my life right now. Plus, when two people are entangled like we were last night, they say things in the heat of passion."

Demoni had a look on his face that I hadn't seen in over 15 years and I hoped that he remembered where we were and kept it cute while in public.

"One thing about me is that I don't say things I don't mean. Tracy, I'm not that same dude that you lost your virginity to back in high school. I am a grown ass man and I know what I want and am very secure about who I am. Can you say the same for yourself?"

If it was my time to kill with my eyes, that moment would have been it.

"Damn, T, I'm sorry I didn't mean it like that. I know that you've been hurt and still healing but I have feelings, as well, and mine are now hurt. We've come a long way and I don't want to lose you this time, but if you're not ready, that's fine. We can just be friends and nothing more."

While he was talking, I listened and finished my food because I was ready to go. People were staring at us, and the last thing he needed was some negative press. I got up once I knew he was finished talking, paid the tab and walked out of the restaurant, waiting for him to pick up his face. I really had no intentions on being rude but what was about to come out my mouth needed to be done in private.

Ten minutes later Demoni came out of Roscoe's looking like someone stole is shoes. He hit the chirp on the car so I could get in and before he could utter a word, I went all the way in.

"First of all, nigga, don't try to make me feel bad about wanting to be single and do my thing. Men do this all the time, finessing women, fucking them and selling BS, and then expecting us to sit and wait around until you're really to be serious."

Not only did he know my situation, we talked about it in bits and pieces and he said he understood; but, all of a sudden, he acting slow. I know I said I needed some time to graduate and get me together; but I'm still flying this plane and no man can make me land until I'm ready to.

"Demoni, I love you from the crown of your head to the corns on your feet…just like I did when we were kids. We have a beautiful 12-year-old daughter and right now is not the right time for me. I'm sorry to disappoint you."

Trying to keep my emotions in check because I was just getting started, "I'm scared baby that If I'm not totally committed to you in a relationship, you'll resent me because I'd be pretending to give you all of me."

As we drove back to my house in silence, my stomach was in knots. I thought I was going to throw up. I turned my body towards the window and cried because I knew there wouldn't be a next time for us. He knew it, too, because he rubbed my back as my shoulders moved up and down in between sobs.

We had some more words after he gathered his travel bag from my bedroom looking all sexy in his sweat suit. And, with his hands in his pocket jiggling the keys, he turned to face me and planted a kiss on my forehead, eyelids and lips one last time.

"Demoni, I'm…"

"Don't say another word, Tracy. I understand now. I love you."

"I love you, too. I swear. I want forever. One day."

Back On The D—Train

Ever meet a guy and asked yourself, "Is he the one?" Every move he seems to make is the right one and you'll do whatever to follow his lead. This is exactly what happened when Derek and I linked up. Funny thing is, we went to school together and never once did I look at him twice. And, not because I thought I was the shit, but because he was never on my radar.

Much to my surprise this man knew more about me than all of the men I've been with combined. Talk about stalker, right? That was my first thought, but when he told me things about myself no one ever pays attention to, I changed my tone quick. He reminded me of nothing more than a fan who admires his or her favorite entertainer.

The first time we made love, he blow my mind and my back out and for once in all my sexual life, I was speechless. I went over to his place which was nice and decorated, as if a woman lived there; but, he assured me he was a bachelor.

"Never been inside a bachelor's pad this spick and span. Who cleans up for you, your mother?"

He laughed at me like I told the funniest joke in the world, "Naw, I always been particular about my house."

I kept looking around at the decor as I followed him through the house. What I immediately observed was that he was very close to his family, as tons of pictures were scattered about. He has a cool little den with a fireplace, a sidebar, flat screen tv and what looks to be his favorite football team all around the room. This was definitely his man cave.

He asked me what I wanted to drink and I opted for a glass of wine. Work had been hectic the first few months. It was Friday and I was down for unwinding.

Derek dimmed the lights and used a remote to turn on some soft music, I guess to set the mood. What a girl move. I was also impressed with the fact that he had candles lit, as well. I could tell he was trying to win the whole tray of brownies and so far, it was working.

Instead of going out for dinner, he ordered some Thai food from this bomb restaurant called Sophie's Kitchen, to make our evening more personal.

We laughed and talked for what seemed to be hours about everything from how we first met, his crush on me since middle school, the passing of his mother and how he was seriously looking for the lady of his life to complete him. I had no idea the night would get so intense and after a few drinks of Moscato, and grown folks' music, I was in a mood. He asked to be excused and since it was his house, I didn't have a say so in the matter. So, while I waited I scanned the room again looking at his music collection, and more pictures I hadn't noticed the first time, all while admiring the beautiful background and people pictured in the photos.

When Derek re-entered the room, he had changed from his jeans and tee shirt to now a bare chest and boy shorts. His brown skin was lean, sculpted and glistening with some type of oil. In his hand was another bottle of wine and a bowl full of fruit. As I looked on, I said to myself, "Oh shit it's about to go down or nah?"

I was flabbergasted at the boldness of how the gears just shifted; but, I was somewhat turned on. I'm glad I had the mind to put on my cute undergarments today, and showered before I came over. He noticed I was staring at him and asked me if I was alright. I quickly relied, "Yes, I'm good," knowing I was slightly on the nervous side. I added a smile for good measures.

"Ok, I'm just making sure, because I don't want you to feel uncomfortable by my sudden come-on."

"You're fine, I guess. I'm a bit shocked just because it was unexpected."

"I can put my clothes back on if you want me to, it's just that the mood has been great up until this point, so I just sorta figured we could...well you know?"

After I finished laughing at his assumption that he was going to automatically get the cookies, I told him that the night was young and if he just slowed down a bit to wait until I caught up, he might get lucky.

I asked him if I could use his bathroom and took my purse with me because I didn't want to be obvious when I began to use my phone. When I reached the bathroom I dialed Selasi's phone and talked as softly as I could in case Derek's walls were thin.

"Girl, why are you whispering?"

"Girl, I'm at Derek's house, and he's in the mood for more than just drinks and talking. What should I do?"

"Give him a little taste but you control the situation, and call me when you get home. Matter of fact, text me his address in case his ass crazy."

I laughed a little louder than expected, texted her real quick, then washed my hands so that it looked as if I really did have to pee. When I came out Derek asked me if everything was ok. I told him it was and that a client called my after-hours line and I needed to take the call. He nodded, poured me another glass and continued to sip on his Whiskey. As he began to take a seat next to me, he planted a soft kiss on my lips and right away my nerve endings started to spark a flame. I put my glass down on the table, moved closer to him, inviting him to give me more.

Damn, he had a great smile and a mouth full of perfect teeth.

I kicked my shoes off, got on top of him not missing a beat with the kisses. Our mouths were doing the tangle with the sweet flavor of my drink and the powerful aftertaste that dark liquor gives off. I made a vow to myself that once I became interested in someone to hang around a person for a while before being sexual, but it's something about Derek that made me want to throw away all my rules. With every dry hump I could feel his manhood harden and his breathing was becoming more labored the deeper we got.

He pulled my shirt over my head so he could snap my bra loose, making my twins hang a bit low but sitting pretty in front of his eyes, which I could tell he approved of.

Since he was already shirtless, I begin to lick every inch of his body from his ears, collarbone, lips, fingertips and kissed his neck and chest. No taco meat for the win, unlike the dirty old men I used to fuck for money.

I started whispering some bullshit in his ears, making him lose control, flipping me off the couch and onto the floor for the dive into my pool. I was purring like a cat, arching my back with every tongue lashing he gave my pond. Just when I was about to see the stars from up above, he told me to turn over and spread. I did as he said, *"Yes, daddy!"* He then laid directly under my pond and had me face-sit until his face was wet. I was now ready for the main event. Not wanting to be a selfish lover I returned the favor by inserting a piece of strawberry in my mouth, chewed it a bit and took his shaft by force with my mouth. As he pumped and pumped inside of me, I could taste the last thing he ate, which meant he was close to blast-off. So, right on cue I stopped and demanded that he fuck me in that very moment.

Body pulsating and going off pure adrenaline, Derek slid to home-run knocking my black bottom from behind, putting me in a trance so far away in a galaxy even NASA wouldn't be able to reach. Now, this is what I could call some bomb love making! He and I forgot the time and explored each other's bodies all over the house until the wee hours of the morning. After I managed to put on my clothes that were now scattered about, I grabbed my things and headed home. I couldn't help but laugh at myself the whole drive, as I rewinded the series of events of how I just had sex with someone I didn't intend to, or did I?

Dammit, being a woman sucks like hell. You meet a cute dude, promise to take things slow and preach about the respect and morals you have for yourself and what do we do ladies? We let a man's charm and good looks persuade you let loose and ride on his horse. Man how sometimes I wish I were a boy.

For about a year straight, Derek and I met up every other Friday for our no strings fling. The only time we didn't hang is if I was on the moon, other prior engagements came up or just to give each other space. The last part was my idea because I couldn't afford to catch feelings while my business was booming. Plus, a small part of me still longed for Demoni. I know...it's sad; but, it's true what they say...in that you never forget your first love. Never.

The *blues has a way,*
a way of bringing out the truth,
feelings, hurt and pain.
So pure with rawness
holding nothing back
like a guitar, crying, begging for your love,
for one more chance
Only for them to
to vanish from your life and to,
never come back, even though,
you want to be saved.

"So, tell me all about Mr. Lova!" Just the thought of my escapade with Derek brings a smile on my face.

"Damn, that good huh, bestie?"

"Let's just say that's how it started, exactly how it is with most guys I've been involved with to-date."

My girls and I came up with an idea when I came back home to stay connected. We valued to spend time together once a month to catch up on life, events coming up and our existing love lives. This works for me because all I do is have discussions with people, except I normally get paid for it. The only difference is when I'm with my girls I get to keep all the way real and not be subjective all the time, or hold back. Sometimes feelings get hurt; but, that's what friends are for. To keep it 100!!!

"Remember the night I called you to ask you what I should do about Derek because we went from hanging out as friends to something else?'

"Yes, go on."

"Well, we let it all hang out and it was well worth it. I had no idea skinny dudes be packing wood."

While I'm telling Selasi how the night went, she was laughing and on the edge of her seat, like she was watching a good suspense movie. Of course I left a few things out but I gave her enough to hold on to. Although I was feeling Derek, something was a little off and at first I couldn't put my finger on it. I wasn't one for making assumptions, so I decided to look out for the red flags that soon began waving. The first six months were great! We went out dancing, movies, we double-dated a few times and I even talked him into joining the gym to workout with me when the girls were too busy to.

One day I'm at home doing laundry and I received a text message from my boy, Earl, playing catch up. I couldn't quite remember when or how he had my number; but, nonetheless, it was Earl.

So about half-way through the day I noticed something. Earl was texting in all caps, and he was being flirty with me, which I didn't understand because he had a girlfriend. Not that him having a girlfriend meant anything because people cheat every day on their partners. Another red flag was another change in the messages. Earl began to say that he heard I was dating his nephew and so I played dumb and asked him who he was talking about. He said, "You know my nephew that is in the Marines."

I went to reply back that that could be anyone, for I knew a few guys who serve our country. I got a "LOL" followed by a cell number.

I looked at the number, trying to figure out why it played a role until something said go through your contacts. Instead of responding to the text because it was clear at this point someone was playing games, I decided to call the number to see what voice I would hear on the other end. Imagine to my surprise – after about three rings – some woman answered.

"Damn, it took you long enough to figure out Earl was not texting you. You must be dumber than I thought and people pay you for advice?"

"First off, let's get something straight. I'm no fool. No man writes in all caps, that's something a petty ass bitch would do."

The whole time I'm talking, she is smackin' and popping damn gum in my ear.

"And furthermore, you have nothing better to do with your time if you know all my business, which is clear that you see me as a threat."

I could not believe that Derek would play me like that. No wonder his house was so clean and we had set times and days that we met up. It didn't bother me at first because we were just kicking it; but, I did begin to wonder, though. He claimed to be so into me but wasn't really trying to invest the time it would take for us to grow a relationship.

I went back and forth with the heffa a few more minutes and suddenly realized I was wasting my time and breathe on a man who didn't belong to me. What I did have were some plans to cuss Derek out, but not before I got some revenge dick. After I got my plans in order, I texted him, telling him how much I missed him and how I couldn't wait until Friday to see him. At first he wasn't down for it but after I sent a short video of me playing with myself, he said he would make some moves in his schedule and pencil me in.

"Ha, is that right?" I got cute and shit, put on a tight dress that revealed everything but what I was about to reveal was going to be epic. Just the day before our meeting I texted his "girlfriend" Tameka and told her where she could meet me to square up because I was not giving up Derek for her. Even though I was sure they were broken up, I was even more sure that he was still fucking her because why else would she go through all the trouble in finding out about me, getting my number and posing as someone else. If she was about *that* life, she would have kept it real from the gate. It's cool, though.

So, instead of our regular Friday rendezvous, Derek and I met on a Wednesday afternoon for a quick bite to eat downtown and then dessert at his house afterwards. I made sure I was being extra touchy and sweet so when shit blew up in his face, he would be looking stupid. Tameka had been blowing up my phone telling me Derek wasn't worth a fight; but wanted to pop up over to the house anyways, so, she, too, could give him a piece of her mind.

I told her I was with it but called my sister for backup, just in case she tried it. After lunch at The Yard House we go back to Derek's, parked our cars and right at the door I pounce on him like a tiger. We start off on the kitchen table going at it rough, almost knocking a hole in the wall. Out the corner of my eye I spot a banana. I unpeel it, smear some on my breast and on his lips. "Damn T, what's gotten in you today?"

"You."

I moved his face close to mine, so I could lick and suck the banana off him all while getting my rocks off for the last time.

"Oh yeah, oh shit, you feel so good baby."

Not wanting to cum too fast he stops and tells me to go upstairs while he grab some whipped cream and the wine. I obeyed, hurried up to text Tameka telling her stay on schedule for the blow up. She replied, "BET."

Derek and I get back to it, until we have no more energy left in us. After about twenty minutes of catching my breath and carrying out my next move, like clockwork my sister called me. I answered it quick sounding all worried and frantic. I could see Derek's eyes on me as he wanted to know what was going on.

"Is everything okay? Who was that, babe?"

Babe... I thought to myself. That was a first, but too bad I couldn't be babe after today. I went through the house like a crazy woman looking for my clothes and explaining to him at the same time that my dad was rushed to the hospital and that I had to go. He asked me if I wanted him to tag along for support and I kindly declined.

"I'll be okay. My family is there waiting on me now. Thank you though."

I turned around and kissed him ever so passionately. Then, the action began. I was expecting Tameka to knock on the door, but no, she had a key! Wow!

"Derek, Derek, baby where are you? I brought you some soup since you said you weren't feeling good enough to go to the Lakers game."

You should have seen the look on his face. He was looking for me, I'm sure; but I hid in his jacket closet next to the kitchen, just before heading out the door.

"Oh, hey baby, you shouldn't have."

"Of course, I did, you're my boo. Besides who else is going to take care of you like me?"

I wanted to laugh so bad but I held it in a little longer because I was still partially undressed. Once I got my arm through my dress and pulled it down and quickly slipped on my shoes, I busted out the closet like a mad woman.

"Oh really, Derek...so this is how we do, huh?"

"Hey, ummm, Tracy, it's not what it look like."

"Derek, who the hell is this, and why was she in the damn closet?"

We both stood between him waiting for him to answer, but nothing came out of his mouth. Tameka and I looked at each other like we were about to fight, then started laughing. Derek was perplexed as to why we were now laughing. You know he had the nerve to get an attitude, but I set his ass straight.

"You know, I was just beginning to like you, but when Tameka started texting me a few days back I figured I'd give you a taste of your own medicine."

"Yep", said Tameka chewing her damn gum. She was ghetto as all outdoors but I must admit she was a cute chick.

"I'm not for the games and I told you that from day one. You played me for a while; but, the game changed on ya ass!"

Tameka added her two cents, grabbed her purse, threw him his keys and sent him to hell and back. I turned to him on my way out the door and said for him not to ever call or text me again. It was then that I knew for sure I would never date again. No matter what I did, I always got stuck with the craziest dudes.

The Jackpot Or Nah?

Now that I am in my prime, I know how to quickly catch men on their bullshit and be real quick to bounce. Why would I put up with unnecessary shenanigans when I know the relationship has no value and that person is not right for me? I have too many home girls who will stick with a man for years because they don't want to be lonely, or he swinging good wood or keep them faded off the purple haze. I've learned that I am enough and if a man can't come to the table with extra for me to eat, then I will starve.

If I need dick that bad, I'll buy a toy. The toys don't upset me, play games or break my heart. Of course, it will NEVER replace the real thing but I refuse to settle; so, until God brings my husband to me, I will gladly be single. Ain't nobody got time for looking old and stressed out over a man who never gave two cents about you.

"Boy, bye!"

Just when I thought my love life was over, I met Marcus! Thank the lord his name starts with a different letter other than D. Perhaps this is a sign and I have finally broke the "situationship" cycle forever. Whatever it means, I'm going to ride the M train until the wheels fall off.

For the first time I am going to use the advice I give my clients and crew about relationships, with hopes I don't screw up. I do tend to overanalyze things because I do it for a living; however, I feel it's important to not turn a blind eye when it comes to men because when you blink - just once - they get yo ass.

Me and the girls were on our usual Friday night happy hour, where we meet and catch up on all the juice or lack thereof for the week. As always, I'm the first one to arrive at our destination when this fine brother with Obama swagger came in. Suit and tie sharp, ray bans perfectly framed for his chiseled face, height of a ladder and ass ample as a pear. I also noticed every other woman in the place checking him out as well, some visually cheating on their men in plain eyesight. I chuckled some by what I had witnessed, never taking my eyes off Mr. GQ and wondering where his woman was, or hell boyfriend, and if he thought he was God's gift to women, or a mama's boy.

He took a seat at the bar clearly waiting for someone and then the door swung open and two gentlemen who looked just like him stepped into, "The Station." Wishing that my girls were here now because I didn't know how much more sexiness I could handle by myself. It was then that I made eye connection with another woman who must have been thinking the same thing. We both gave each other that, "Girl, aren't they fine" look, and laughed as if we'd known each other. Just when I was about to become restless by the tardiness of CP time, my sister, Nivea, walked in – all out of breath and talking way too fast.

"Take ya time, Niv…you straight. Hold our spot, though, because I need to tinkle. Oh, and order some drinks while I'm away."

She quickly hugged and kissed me and sat down, but not before she picked up the drink menu.

Oh shit, I had to go pass the bar where the three amigos in suits were sitting, before I reached the ladies room. I did a quick scan of their bodies from head to toe and made sure at least one of them saw me walking.

"Thank God I wore this dress" I muttered to myself, walking all extra hard like. After doing my thang, and reapplying my lipstick, I walked closer to my bait almost on purpose but not really, only to get stopped by a pair of big soft hands grabbing my forearm. Caught, like a fish on a hook!

"Dang girl, I see you with all this ass up in here."

Immediately I was turned off and made a face to match it. Nasty dog licking his lips as if he left his manners at home.

"I'm sorry, Miss, Jerod sometimes gets too excited around the ladies. My name is Marcus, Marcus Ingram."

Marcus was actually the one I wanted anyways, Mr. GQ.

"Hello, Mr. Ingram, Tracy Porter, nice to meet you. Gentlemen", I stated to the thirst bucket, Jerod, and Floyd, the other gentleman who seemed to be the shyer one of the three.

"So, Marcus, my name is Nivea and I'm Tracy's sister. She single and ready to mingle, and by the way she looking at you cause she already likes you."

My sister has embarrassed me before but this time was by far the worse and how did she get over to the other side of the bar so damn quick?

Selasi was no help either sipping on her drink co-signing. Just like in Ms. Largo's class I was called out. Sweating underneath my hair and nervous as all hell because I didn't know if this man was married, gay, had a girlfriend or had baby mama drama.

"Let me see your phone."

Marcus was a little reluctant at first but figured my sister was harmless.

"Ok, I just programed her number in your phone so make sure you call or text her later."

"I'm so sorry, Marcus, for my sister's behavior."

"It's quite alright, beautiful. She made it easy for me."

He was laughing at the show the girls were putting on; but, I felt like the butt of the joke. What was done was done now. The rest of the night went well. I got to know quite a bit about Marcus in the short time we spent at the bar. He had me laughing, and while I was occupied, Niv and Selasi kept the other fellas company. From the looks of it, they, too, were having a great time. I had no idea that I would find my enchanted love that night, but I thank God that we found one another because I was starting to believe I was cursed.

After getting past the first stages of trying to see if we were a fit, it was smooth sailing from there. Marcus and I had so much in common from music, working out, our favorite food being fried chicken, traveling the world and being family oriented. My favorite feature of his were his eyelashes. They were long and curly and when he got sleepy his eyes sparkled.

Everything about him is what any woman would want in a man. He was not only smart and funny, he was attentive to all my needs. He was the ying to my yang and everything with him was so simple.

I never had to ask for anything. He was compromising in every sense of the word and when I was being complicated, he was the most patient person in the world. We waited months before having sex, because we both agreed that it would get in the way of really getting to know each other.

He had so much fun together and because we stayed busy, sex was usually the last thing on our minds. For the first time I was truly in love. The only thing I was having a problem with was whether or not to disclose information about my past and the lifestyle I use to live. I mean what if he judged me based on that, or treated me differently?

Hell even my clients made comments on how much different I seemed to be. My assistant noticed it first.

"Girl, who and what has gotten into you? You all glowing and everything, Dr. T!!"

I tried to pretend as though I had no idea what she was talking about. "I think it's due to me sleeping better, I just bought new mattresses."

"Yeah right, you've been sleeping all right and not by yourself. You've got a love on top honey, what's his name?"

I could no longer deny it, so I busted out with laughter, "His name is Marcus Ingram."

"Yasss girl, I knew it!! Thanks for the raise by the way."

"I gave you a raise, Gina?"

"Really?"

"I'm just playing. You do great work here and for that I can afford to pay you more for your services. Who's coming in next?"

Gina flipped the book to the next page that revealed a new client by the name of Mario Johnson.

The first time Marcus and I were intimate, it was like being a virgin all over again, except I knew what I was doing. It wasn't just sex, or fucking like the young folks do. But some real live love making. Never seeing *"Love Jones"* (before Marcus agreed it watch it with me) to see why I loved the movie so much. We began with popcorn, candy, wine and candles all over the living room. About half way through the movie Marcus grabbed my right hand and began to plant small kisses on them; and, as much as I wanted to see the movie to the end, I couldn't. A fire had started and it needed to be put out.

The candles and Merlot were the cause of it all. He let the movie continue to play on silent, got on the floor and removed my fuzzy socks. He proceeded to massage my feet, then my calves, thigh meat and then stopped. He told me to take off all my clothes and open wide. Not quite sure where the oil came from but he poured it on my bush and played in the garden until it became wet. My stomach, arms and breast were next for touching and no longer being able to contain myself I started to squirm a bit; but, Marcus took his time. He then told me to stay on the sofa but get on my knees. Obeying the captain, I did as I was told. The candles were doing a dance and so was my body on the inside.

After he lathered up my neck and back, he saved the very best for last. Already wet, I suddenly felt a piece of ice insert between the crack of my ass then inside my hot spot. He massaged me again but with his long tongue, and I rode his face until I couldn't take any more. He led me into the bedroom, which also was set up. Damn he was good, I thought. *"When did he have time to do this and where was I at?"* It didn't even matter at that point because it was going down, and I was ready for whatever he had in store.

I watched as he removed every article of clothing like he was a stripper, never losing eye contact with me. His body was perfect, so long and lean with muscles all in the right place. I was aching and he knew it whispering in my ears, "We got all night baby." I just wanted to scream, take me now daddy, but I followed his lead. We kissed like wild beasts and with every inch I took him all in, filling up my cream pie with his warmth. He stroked me slow and hard at first, then fast with a little roughness. Our hands were intertwined, eyes meeting every chance we got and holding on to each other as if one of us was going to be taken away. This went on it seemed like all night until I realized I was cold, which was because we were on top of the sheets and naked.

My head was spinning and my body was tingling with electrons from the amazing love making that just happened a few hours ago. That night, for sure, I knew I was truly in love and nothing was going to tear us apart. He was mine for the taking. From that point forward it was like us against the world, nothing else mattered; and, for a while we abandoned everything and everyone but our professions. Our friends and families would call and text us to hang out; but, we declined each time because he were enjoying one another and didn't want to share just yet. After a year of dating, we decided to take our relationship to the next level.

"Babe, let's move in together."

"Are you sure you want to do this, Marcus? You know I have a daughter and before I agree with that, I need to discuss this with her first and see how her father feels about it. Once I get the green light, then we can proceed."

He was listening to me with a blank stare but how he responded to what I had just said would also determine the type of man I was really dealing with.

One thing was for certain, my daughter thought he was great and liked that he made me happy and did things for her as well. I made it very clear that Marcus was not replacing her dad nor did I love her any less because he occupied my time. The talk with Sydney and her father was easier than I expected and I couldn't wait to share the news with babe.

"Mom, I love you and want to see you happy. You have been through a lot and deserve only the best."

Then Demoni chimed in saying he agreed and that he approved but wanted to meet with Marcus for obvious reasons. And just like a typical teen, Sydney blurted out that she was going to have two dads instead of one. Although Demoni laughed at her comment, I know he kept his true feelings to himself for the sake of our daughter.

Before leaving the house with his sad eyes, he planted forehead kisses on me and Sydney then grabbed his keys to exit.

"Alright, ladies, glad we had this talk; but, I have an early flight tomorrow."

We walked him through the door and to the car, hugged as usual and said our goodbyes. Once Sydney was no longer in ear shot, Demoni and I had a little more to say to one another.

"Whatever you need, babe, let me know. I'm here no matter what."

"I know and I thank you for all you do for our family."

He just gave me a little smile and drove away. I couldn't wait to see Marcus again to go over the details of how this move was going to work. We decided to meet at our favorite spot at the Marina Del Rey.

"So, which one of us are going to move, or should be buy in together?"

Apparently, he and I were on the same page. I, however, didn't care just as long as we were together. After a few minutes of silence he said he was okay with moving into my place, so that Sydney wouldn't feel she was being displaced. So, it was settled. I helped him pack the things that were coming to my place; and, he either donated or sold some of the things he no longer had a need for. He had some great things, too, that the Salvation Army and the local shelters were going to love. Just one more reason to move in with him. Marcus Ingram was perfect!!!

If I knew love was going to be like this
I would have found you sooner.
you make me a better me
forgetting about all the others. Everything I went through before
was preparation for now.
all I wear is a smile,
for all you've done was light up my world.
no one can take the place of my King
I love you now, and forever
and "yes" I'll be your Queen!

Dr. Porter

Anne Baxter was her name – my first client. At five-eight and a half, a school principal who had never been in a real relationship with a man, only situationships, she was beyond fed up and had almost given up hope of having her own family...until she made an appointment after driving by my office out of desperation for guidance.

"Good morning, Ms. Baxter, I'm Dr. Porter; but, you can call me Tracy, if it makes you more comfortable."

"Thank you, but I prefer to be professional until we've gotten to know one another more."

"That's fine, and what would you like me to call you?"

I could tell she was a little uncomfortable, because she was fidgeting a bit and wasn't quite sure how to position herself on the couch.

"Anne."

"Anne, can I get you some coffee, water or tea? And if you'd like, you can take off your jacket and shoes if it helps."

She gave me a smile and a chuckle. "It's that obvious, huh?"

"Let me put it to you this way. I want you to think of me as one of your girlfriends and we are just hanging out. I assure you that you'll get the best service today and there is nothing to worry about."

Her shoulders began to relax and her breathing became less labored.

"Thank you for the pep talk. This is my first time talking to a stranger about my most intimate affairs."

We went back and forth a few more minutes, going over my credentials, the way I like to lead the sessions and the importance of coming to resolutions that best fit her. The main objective being that she has to be open to putting in the work; otherwise, time and money will be wasted on her end.

The first two sessions were about me getting a backstory on Anne and the main reason she decided she wanted to seek counsel. Anne was a 42-year-old Spanish American whose parents met when dating outside their race was frowned upon. Her mother migrated from Mexico to Los Angeles in the late fifties and her father was a Marine. The two met at the base, where her mother was a shy and pretty cleaning lady trying to find her way in the US.

Her father, Erik Baxter, just so happened to report to the very building Anne's mother worked in. It was love at first sight but there was something stopping their love affair. Selena Gomez spoke Spanish primarily so verbal communication was a bit challenging; but, the two didn't give up until they broke the ice. Erik began to learn enough Spanish to claim his prize and Selena worked overtime to learn the English language.

After a few years of courting the two married and settled in Anaheim, California, where Anne and her brother, David, lived most of their lives.

Anne explained how life was great and how ever so often they went to Disneyland until the unthinkable happened. Dad was separated from the family from time to time, due to deployments; and, her mother became withdrawn and picked up a nasty habit of drinking, due to being lonely without their father. For years she said it bothered her because she didn't think her mother loved her. Her brother got most of the attention and she got yelled at for no reason.

"She would tell me she was harder on me because I was the oldest and she wanted me to be stronger, and smarter than she was", Anne said.

"So, you didn't think she loved you because she was hard on you?"

She went on to tell me there was more to the story like how David was a splitting image of their father so he got the hugs, kisses and the love; whereas, Anne had chores to do and helped out with dinner. I asked her about her grandparents and her mother's upbringing, but she had nothing for me because her mother never spoke of them. Then, when her father came back from duty she would change up, pretending like everything was great.

"I knew it was a stunt, Dr, Porter, and played along for the sake of my father; but, it was uncomfortable and of course fake."

While listening to her story and watching her body language and changes in her voice, I was jotting down notes trying to piece together where I thought future sessions would take us.

"Ms. Baxter, thank you for being open and doing the work. This is the end of session one."

"Already? Boy does time go by fast. So, what's next?"

"If you think I am the right person for you, make an appointment with Gina in the front for what day or days suit you and we'll pick up from there. The goal is to connect from your past to now and figure out what brought you here today and find some resolutions."

"Ok, Dr. Porter, I understand how this works. Thank you, again, for your time and I'll see you soon."

I let her out the office with a warm hug and gave her my after-hours number, in case of an emergency. I was so sure that after our session I wouldn't see her again.

Believe it or not people expect to get all the answers or have their issues fixed the first session and it just doesn't work that way. Most importantly I want clients to know I am doing a service that I take pride in because I love what I do, not to mention having to put my social life on pause to make sure I was the best of the best coming out of college. And of course dear old daddy's coins that helped me open my own firm.

Within my first two years I had ten clients. Business was booming, thanks to word of mouth, the networking I do, as well as the education I was provided with to help me during my humble beginnings. Two weeks later after Anne and I had our first session she came back. I wasn't so sure at first; because like most people, they don't think a shrink can help them with their personal problems. For starters we're strangers to them and know nothing about them and they may feel uncomfortable. However, what they forget is that they sought me out for counsel.

Now while I get why people are apprehensive in the beginning, the fact is that we're perfect people for help because there are no biases going in, and we can look at the situation from a subjective point of view. We are trained to not be judgmental even though the stories we hear have us subconsciously laughing at the stupidity and silently cursing them out for not seeing the obvious.

"Ms. Baxter, so good to see you."

"Doctor Porter, boy am I glad to see you." She took off her coat and shoes all in one beat and seemed much more relaxed and ready to lay her burdens down a lot quicker than the first time she visited my office.

"Well, why don't you get settled and we can jump right in."

"May I have a cup of tea first?"

"Sure, I'll pour you a glass. Would you like honey, or sugar?"

"Both please."

I made her a cup from the fresh pot of brewed tea, which was still very hot and brought about a sweet aroma in the office. For a few minutes I sat silently with my notes open to where we last left off. I asked her if she wanted to begin where we left off or the real reason she was seeking counsel. She wasted no time telling me she was having issues with her man.

"So, my man, Clyde, and I have been together for almost four years and he won't fully commit."

"And you've been alright with this for this long because?"

"I really don't know. That's where you come in at, doc."

I scratched my neck and shifted in my seat some, so that I could come to grips with what she just said.

"Ok, let's start with how you two met, what attracted you to him and then as the story moves on, I'll ask more questions."

Anne went on about how the two of them met at the gym, which she claims was love at first sight. They played cat and mouse for a few weeks until Clyde decided to approach her. Having just ended a relationship she was not all in at first, but because he was good looking and she had her eye on him for some time, she figured why not exchange digits.

As the story moved along, she talked about the honeymoon phase where the sex was amazing, the long talks and walks were like the corny romance movies we all have watched. She was like an excited teenager who found puppy love and then after twenty minutes the story shifted completely.

"Let me stop you here, Anne. From where I stand, Clyde seems to be all that and then some. So, tell me where the two of you are at now."

With all the eye rolling, hair flipping and heavy sighing, she went into how she asked him to move in to take the relationship to another level.

"He flat out told me right now was not the right time."

"How long ago did the two of you have this talk?"

"Six months ago."

"Now, I want you to think for me, Anne. Has his behavior changed any?"

"Come to think of it, he has been acting weird for some time now. Right after I came back from visiting family in New York a year ago, I noticed he wasn't as attentive as before, which was weird. If you knew us, you would know we couldn't stand being apart. He seemed to be a lot more busy than usual and not staying the night after sex."

"Did you ever mention to him the change you discovered, and if so, what was his response?"

"He became defensive and making excuses for what he claimed I was doing. He said if I couldn't handle his busy schedule to let him know because we could end the relationship now. All I was trying to do was get an understanding as to how our relationship shifted all of a sudden and the best thing was to ask rather than assume. After her calmed down he apologized for getting amped up and said work was stressing him because he really wanted to make partner at his firm. I told him I understood and that if that was it, he could have just said that. After all we had been dating for four years already. We knew each other's friends and family, so I thought everything was on point.

"Ok, interesting! Now because we are now out of time let me stop you here. However I want to give you a little homework and think about this. What if there is another woman, or man even? Pay close attention to his body language and bring up the moving in once more. Come back for your next visit with your findings and then I will give you the final conclusion and what you should do."

"OMG, Doctor. You don't think he's cheating, do you?'

As she was on the verge of tears I held her in my arms, told her to breathe and not assume. I simply wanted her to think about the possibility, due to what I've assessed. I walked her to the front desk where Gina was sitting, so she could book her next appointment. I thanked her for her service, went back into my office to add more notes and full assessment in her file. I had just enough time to eat really quick and brush my teeth before my next client came in…Mario Johnson!

For about six months Mario has been coming to my office trying to find himself. His case is a wee bit unique because he's attracted to both men and women, which is half of the world now-a-days. So, when Mario was seven he was molested by his teenaged babysitter, Brian, who his mother trusted in his care while she worked the overnight shift at the hospital. He never told a soul about what happened to him, like most children who are afraid people won't believe them. He – instead – suppressed the memories and went on with his life.

As a result he found himself liking boys, and then men (after a while) because of what happened to him. Somewhere in his mind he found that it was normal to be bisexual and for years Mario battled with his demons and indecisiveness of which sex he wanted to be with the most. Like most of us, we were told that it was a sin to be gay and lesbian and so Mario fights the feelings between right and wrong. Not wanting to shame his family, he has put on a mean front.

"So, Mario, what is the latest? The last time we met you were living sort of a double life. You have a girlfriend named, Trina, and when the urges rise, you seek attention from men. Is this behavior still going on?"

As he sits across from me on the couch looking fine as he wanna be, he crosses and uncrosses his legs, which is a clear indicator not much has changed. He's gathering his thoughts.

"You see, doc, what I get from women is different from a man."

"Okay, elaborate."

"Well, with women they provide their beauty, soft skin, great conversation and, no disrespect, but wet pussy and their nurturing." He laughed after saying that, and I wanted to slap him but I would be acting unprofessional.

"That's it?"

"No, there's more. But when I'm with men, I'm in control… empowered, if that's a better word. The touch is different. We have more in common, I feel, and it seems to be less drama for me."

Before I began to speak, I finished up my notes, sipped my afternoon tea and went in.

"Ok, so what I gathered from what you've just said was that you like women because they are feminine and sexually desirable. Does it not matter that women are also smart and bring a lot to the table?"

I continued by saying, "Would it be also safe to say that the men you choose are more submissive?"

Mario gave me a puzzled look.

"Is this by choice or does it just happen like that?"

I asked him all of these questions because I feel that he dates women because the bible says it's an abomination to be with a man and he doesn't want to shame his family. And, due to being molested by a male, he's trying to figure out if he's attracted to men by nature or only doing it to take back the control he lost when his innocence was taken away from him.

"Do you think what happened to you has anything to do with why you're here seeking professional help"?

Mario let me finish what I had to say before interjecting.

"I love how you keep it real and can read into the littlest information provided."

I wanted to say duh, that's why I get paid the big bucks. But in all seriousness Mario needs to pick not a side so-to-speak; but, just one person to love, so that no one gets hurt. Trina deserves to know the truth, which I'm having a hard time understanding how she doesn't already know. For starters his eyebrows are arched, nails are super clean and he wears his pants tighter than most men. In addition to that, his mannerisms are a bit woman-like, but maybe she's into that.

"So, have you told Trina?"

"That's why I'm really here today. She's pregnant! And while I'm happy I'm going to be a father I met someone I really like; but, I'm not sure how my telling her about Trent will stress her and the baby out."

"How far along is she?"

As I waited for him to give me his answer, I could tell he was happy.

"Just 16 weeks."

I asked his how long has he been with Trent, where they met and how did he know he was sure about his feelings towards a man at this time. He went on to say how they met at the gym during spin class one night, and how they'd been giving each other the eye for a while but neither acted upon it. They started out just meeting for lunch and he found that each time he would get butterflies in his stomach. They talked about everything under the sun and how Trent was the first person he told about being molested. And come to find out, Trent had the same experience except it was a women who took away his innocence.

"Now that I know how he makes me feel I have no choice but to tell Trina the truth, not just for the sake of our child; but, because she deserves to know."

Of course as soon as the sessions begin to get juicy the bell goes off.

"Well, Mr. Johnson, that is our time. I will suggest that you bring Trina to the next session if you'll feel more comfortable. In that way, I can provide the support you'll need just in case things go sour. He was so elated that I offered that, he gave me a really big and long hug. It was a little too nice for comfort, and I almost got moist. He smelled good.

Nothing Ever Lasts Forever

You came into my life
For just a little while, and
Then you disappeared.
Although a part of me died when you
Left my side, you came back to me in
A form of a rainbow.
Always smiling at me through the heavens.

I've been through hell and back, pushed through the rough patches and got myself all the way together, just to have it taken away from me. I'm more empty than ever before. Marcus had been complaining about his stomach for some time now, and each time I mentioned the word doctor he shot me down...until that one unforgettable night, that is.

Our Saturday fun day started off as usual with breakfast, a quick workout session and the movies. When we first began dating, we spent countless hours talking about any and everything, and movies was top of the list. To my surprise Marcus was a hopeless romantic and turned into a big kid every time a new comedy was premiering. In the past I would go to the movies with my girls; but, I must say I enjoyed hanging with my babe. Plus, there's nothing like making out in the dark at the movies. Corny, right? Well, I'm a late bloomer so I take it as a conquered objective on my bucket list.

Later on that evening my friend, Netise, was hosting a party to celebrate passing the BAR. This is when our night became turbulent.

"Babe I'm going to take a quick nap before we head out, okay?"

He made this face like the pain was too unbearable, yet offered me a quick smile ensuring that he was fine.

"Probably just some gas, again, not to worry."

He quickly kissed me, showered and was snoring before I could count to five. The whole time at the party Marcus was quiet...too quiet! He loved to laugh and make jokes with people, no matter if he knew them are not. Being that he's an investment broker, he was not shy. All night he kept smiling, balling up his fist to fight whatever pain he was feeling and in the name of LOVE.

Since I was a psychiatrist, I knew – at that moment – he didn't have indigestion and I was worried. Feeling bad about dragging him to the party, I made my way through to say goodbye to my friends, found Netise, and told her we were leaving.

"Why are you leaving, you just got here?"

She was already on glass number three of whatever cocktail and was well on her way to Drunkville.

"Girl, we've been here for over two hours, plus we had a long day and I have to hit it so I can make it to morning service."

We did our hug and kiss ritual and promised to text her when I got home, knowing she wouldn't see it until late afternoon.

Marcus became elated when I told him we were leaving, so he could rest. "Thanks, babe."

We didn't talk much on the ride back like we normally would after attending a function. As a matter of fact, Marcus fall asleep while I was driving. Soon as he realized we were home, he quickly ran upstairs, took off his clothes and made a dash for the bathroom. He was in there so long I was able to shower, wash a few dishes in the sink and text Netise, "HOME".

"Are you okay, I yelled. Do you need anything?"

When he didn't answer that's when I knew it was serious; so, I put on a pair of jeans, my college sweatshirt and Uggs. I then told Marcus after he was finished to get dressed so we could go to the hospital. A few more minutes of silence and what I seen after opening the door was frightening enough to make a horror movie. There was vomit all over the place. Marcus was sweating and crying at the same time.

In between sobs he was trying to tell me to get out and I ignored his request. When he got off the commode it was piled up for days and that's not the worse part. His poop was red. I pushed the image out my mind, took off all my clothes and began running water to clean him up. I helped him into the hot tub full of jets and bathed him just as his mother did when he was a child. As much as I wanted to cry, I stayed strong because from what I could see, he was going to need me. In the few minutes of silence that seemed like forever I said a silent prayer. "Jesus, give me the strength to be both the friend and woman Marcus needs to overcome whatever this mess is in his body. And I cover Marcus in your blood and I need him to have faith and believe everything will be alright. In the mighty name of Jesus, I pray. Amen!"

I dressed Marcus the best I could; because, at this point he was just too weak to do much. The 15-minute drive to the hospital, I swear, seemed to have taken more like 30; but, we made it. I drove my truck to the emergency area, quickly parked close and then, like a baby, I sat in my truck and cried. it didn't last too long, though, because what he was experiencing was worse than my tears.

After having to wait a while for Marcus to be checked in and doctors to run a bunch of tests, I managed to call his boys, Jared and Floyd, booked a flight for Mr. and Mrs. Ingram, and sent Gina to pick them up and bring them to King Drew hospital promptly. When we were finally able to see Marcus, my stomach was queasy. I decided to let his friends go in first because I was too afraid of what I was going to see and hear. Jared went in first and quickly came out saying he just couldn't do it, seeing his buddy laid up in the hospital especially when Marcus was the strongest and healthiest of the trio.

As soon as I was about to comfort him, in came Mrs. Ingram and Nivea. Poor lady looked like she hadn't eaten in days and her stride was slow and weak. When she laid eyes on Floyd, she burst into tears, hugged him for dear life and motioned for me to do the same.

"What happened to my baby, Tracy?"

I briefly told her the series of events that day, which ultimately led us to the hospital and how we've just been allowed to see him. She let go of both myself and Floyd, kissed Jared on the cheek and went in the room. Now, I felt I was ready to go in but decided to let Claudette and Marcus have a private moment. Waking from a nap Marcus, with tears in his eyes, whispered to his mother and reached an arm out to her, letting her know she was needed.

As tired as I was at four a.m., I was not leaving my man's side; and, against my better judgment, fell asleep in one of those hard chairs at the hospital, only to wake with a migraine and a sore neck. After a few tests were ran, the doctor informed us that Marcus had what I feared the most, "Cancer."

"But, he eats all the basic food groups, takes his vitamins religiously and works out like an athlete."

"I understand, Ms. Porter, but cancer is tricky and I've seen other patients just like Mr. Ingram."

He went on to say that they were going to do an emergency surgery to rid of the cancer cells located in his abdominal area, keep him for a few days and discuss life expectancy as well as treatment options. I swear to you all of what he said sounded like a foreign language and nothing made any sense. I just nodded so Dr. Willaby would shut up.

Marcus had been sedated, so he was in and out of consciousness; but, I must have kissed him a thousand times, whispering over and over how much I loved him. And even though he never verbally said a thing, the squeeze of his hands said enough.

Jerod took my hand and led me to the cafeteria where we went to get coffee. For an hour he told me the sweetest and craziest stories about how he and Marcus met. We both laughed and cried so much that snot was running down our faces. We all decided that once the surgery was over, we'd go to my house, nap and freshen up before returning back to the hospital.

I've been to a few funerals in my lifetime; but this one, if Marcus does not make it, will be a hard one for me – for sure. Of course, Mr. and Mrs. Ingram would stay at my house for as long as they needed to, out of support of their one and only son. They each tried to tell me without being rude that they would stay at a hotel; but, I quickly put a stop to it, saying Marcus wouldn't want it any other way.

"We're family, Mrs. Ingram, and I love every single fiber of your son; therefore, you must stay with me. Plus, I need you, just as much as you need me right now."

I gave her a warm smile and a hug that she so desperately needed. She couldn't refuse me after that.

"She's right, Claudette. Right now is not the time to be hard headed."

After realizing that she lost the battle she just nodded, went back into Marcus' room to retrieve her purse and we all walked down the hallway of the hospital that seemed to never end.

After about a week, Marcus was back at home with the around-the-clock care, because he was still very weak. Dr. Willaby gave us some news none of us wanted to hear.

"So, because of the advance stages of this cancer, we weren't able to remove all of the cancerous cells. He has a chance of going into remission and beating this thing with chemo and going on a strict diet. Or, worse case scenario, he has anywhere between four to six months to live."

I thought we were all going to die at that moment; but, we had to be strong for Marcus and stay prayerful. Mr. Ingram left after a few days to take care of business, while Claudette stayed in Los Angeles with me for a month. I thanked God every day for them both, and of course my girls, Jared and Floyd. Without those people I would have been a nut basket, trying to maintain my business and being a supportive girlfriend and nurse for Marcus after the nurses left for the day.

Marcus was very standoffish with me at first, wanting nothing more than his mommy, as if he were a little boy with a common cold. Although I totally understood in the beginning, I began to feel he resented me, as if I was the one who gave him the awful disease. Especially since I was his ride-or-die from the moment I realized something was wrong in the bathroom that God-awful night. His mother explained to me that he was afraid, and felt like less than a man. He didn't know how to be on the receiving end of being cared for because he was so used to being the giver. Even though I understood, I had to remind him we were in this together and God allowed us to meet for a reason. I was here for the ride until it ended.

"Babe, come here so I can talk to you with yo fine ass." I blushed as usual whenever he spoke to me naughty.

I gently stroked his face and kissed him ever so softly.

"Yes, babe, what is it?"

He sighed long and heavy, moved his body as best as he could, then grabbed my hand before he spoke again.

"You know I love you, and I'm so sorry if I've been so distant since coming home."

I tried to cut in but he shut me down, saying that no matter what he was going through he had no right to be rude and insensitive.

"You've had my back since the very beginning of this ordeal and if you hadn't been here two months ago, bathed me and rushed me to the hospital, there is no telling how much worse I would have been. I may have died that night. You saved my life and for that I owe you."

As much as I've tried to push that night out of my head, I would never forget it, as long as I live.

"I understand, Marcus. When you love someone, you'll do just about anything to show them how much – through sickness and in health, the good and the bad."

"My mother told me I was being somewhat selfish and I needed to apologize to you, so let me, damn it."

We both laughed a little but not without him coughing some. At that very moment I wished I could make love to him and ride him into the sunset; but doctors' orders were not to, at least not right now.

"I want you to know that when I'm gone, do not mourn for long because you have too much life to live and I want you to be happy."

Not wanting to think about not having him in my life brought me to tears with serious knots in my stomach. How was I going to deal with this? Would I ever love again?

"Don't worry about me. Just focus on getting better and beating this cancer, so we can plan the rest of our lives."

We both knew the outcome; but, because we were believers and had faith, that's what we're going to stand on until God said otherwise.

Once a week I took off from my practice to be with Marcus for his chemotherapy; and, even though he was weak from treatment, he found a way to stay strong and positive. It even seemed as though he was getting better, or at least that's what I wanted to believe. The truth was that he was losing more and more weight by the minute. And not that I was fat, but I, too, was losing weight from stressing over him and not taking care of myself. Floyd began to take notice and stepped in when he had free time to give me a break. And when he wasn't available, Jerod came through, cooking and taking Marcus out for some air. And then the worse day of my life happened. Marcus and I went out for some ice cream and movies for our date night I had planned at home.

It started out with his favorite dishes, fried chicken, cabbage, a garden salad, cornbread, macaroni and cheese and deviled eggs. I even added an element of surprise by having the fellas drop by and my girls, as well.

"Dang, girl, you sure made a lot of food for just you and me."

I smiled defiantly because he had no idea what was up my sleeve. The doorbell rang, and as he was finishing his next sentence people were walking in the house and music all of a sudden was being played. Marcus wore the biggest smile of his life and tears started to form out of pure happiness and surprise. I also seen a halo over his body in which I knew this would be his last day on earth.

His parents were to fly in the next morning for their visit with him; but I didn't tell him because I thought for sure he'd have more time. For one night, Marcus was his old self, talking about old times and making us laugh about everything and then nothing at all. Once the crew left, I ran bath water with candles, bubbles and jazz music for the both of us in a farewell romantic night.

"Marcus, darling, your bath is waiting for you. Get in and I'll meet you in a few minutes."

Knowing me all too well, he asked what was up my sleeve. I tried to contain myself the best I could. I lied, telling him nothing, but not without a grin on my face. "Mmm hmm, have I told you I loved you today?"

"No, but we had a busy day. Now, get in the tub before the water gets cold."

He obeyed me, moving slow and as careful as he could. A few minutes later I came in with my hair in a high ponytail, naked with my pumps on and two flutes for champagne. In the beginning we just sat holding each other as Nina Simone cooed in our ears. Then I turned around and straddled him asking him if he had one last wish, what it would be. He cupped each side of my face, kissed me hard and said he wanted to make love to me one more time. I reminded him that it might not be a good idea. He didn't care because he was living out his last wish and wanted to die a happy man. Plus, he said, nothing was wrong with his manhood and he needed to release.

Although I was a wee bit nervous, I didn't want to disappoint and even hoped that that night I would get pregnant. I purposely left the condoms in the room, and I think he knew it, too, because he never asked me to get them before we started.

My heart was racing fast but I didn't let him know it. I sat my gold mine onto his shaft and he quickly swelled up filling me up and I pumped until our rhythm matched. The candles began to flicker due to the water splashing but Marcus held on tight, kissing me wildly in the water that was cold. I helped him out the tub and we walked together kissing and holding hands until we made it to the bed. I gently helped him lay down, then took him by mouth to get him ready for the next round. He stopped me mid-way and told me to put my mound on his face and ride until he couldn't take anymore. Not wanting to deter him of his wish, I did so happily until I came. Out of nowhere he all of a sudden had the strength of incredible hulk, flipping me over and taking me in like never before. Out of breath I managed to say, "Be careful, babe."

As if in another world he gave me all he had, then we both hit the high note panting. Energy zapped for sure.

As I lay on his chest, he help me close until we both fell asleep. At about three a.m., nature was calling and I couldn't ignore the fact that I had to tinkle. I hurried because it was cold, and I was naked feeling better than I ever had in months. What I quickly noticed was that Marcus was not snoring like he usually does and he never moved from his position. It was then I knew.

Mr. and Mrs. Ingram's flight was due to arrive at seven a.m.; but, sadly, it was too late to say goodbye to their beloved Marcus. Not wanting to fall apart at that very moment, I decided to clean up the mess Marcus and I made the night before. I dressed him again, the best I could and covered his body with the pillows propped as if he were just sleeping.

I had my driver go pick the Ingram's' up from LAX, while I got myself together to call Jared, Floyd, the girls, my baby girl, Demoni and my parents to let them all know Marcus died in his sleep. When the doorbell rang this time, there were no smiles, just sadness.

"Mom, what are you doing here. I wasn't expecting you, just yet." She held me, told me to just be quiet and the tears begin to fall like a river. Still standing in front of my door, Mrs. Ingram rushed to our side and whispered, "He's gone, isn't he?"

There was no easy way to say it; but, being that she was a mother she already knew. She screamed, "Why, Lord, why?"

Mr. Ingram was not far behind, consoling his wife; but, he was no better. Together they both went upstairs to say goodbye to a man who was once a boy and that they had raised to be an extraordinary person. Just like the day before, my house was filled with people crying out loud and silently to both mourn and celebrate the life of Marcus Lee Ingram.

After the corners took him away, everything from there was pretty much a blur and would be for a while. The home going was beautiful, Marcus looked so peaceful and I was glad he was no longer in pain. Every time I had a dream about Marcus, I swear I could smell is cologne and feel him next to me in our bed. I would reach out for him just to wake up in cold sweats holding onto the pillow on his side of the bed.

I realized that I hadn't changed my bedding since Marcus passed, but doing so would be erasing the memories and I wasn't ready to let go yet. I wanted to keep him and the memories alive as long as I could. Six months went by and the doors to my office were still closed and I wasn't sure if I would ever go back to work. The most I'd done for sure was wake up, cry, eat junk food, surf the net and go back to sleep.

Nivea, Selasi, Mom and Dad dropped by the house once a week to try and cheer me up. Some days were good, other days were not. We've even gotten in verbal squabbles.

"Tracy, now enough is enough!" Dad had the nerve to say one day, "It's been six months and Marcus would not..."

Stopping him in mid-sentence, "Who are you to tell me how long to grieve?"

Unable to control myself, going from 0 to 100 real quick. In all the years Dad and I haven't had an argument since my running away with Demoni and that was almost fifteen years ago. You should have seen the expression on his face when I went off on him. He had no idea how it felt to lose someone. First, it was he and my mom's attempt to force Sydney into adoption, and me being without Demoni for the sake of their reputation.

Everyone had gotten used to me being so picture perfect; but, for once, I wanted to feel like a normal person...like my ass needed psychiatric evaluation. After years of kissing frogs, I had finally found the perfect man for me. And what happened? He gets diagnosed with cancer and I had to watch him wither away and there was nothing I could do.

No matter how much of an expert I was in my field, none of what I've learned during class and with my clients was helping me at all. And people want to put a time on how long I can mourn?!!

"Fuck them!"

Moving On

For the first time ever in all the years I've been a therapist, I can now say I can relate to my clients. The one-year anniversary of Marcus' departure from life was around the corner and the hurt and pain I felt still had me hopeless, and afraid to open my heart to any other man. I was being unfair to my daughter and neglecting her needs to the point that I felt it was only right to let Demoni care for her full time.

I used to tell my women clients that the best way to get over a man is to find another one, a better version of the one you lost, who is going to treat you like the queen that you are. I'll never repeat those words again as long as I have breath in me, because as much as I want to get through this and be happy, I just want my love back. And anyone other than Marcus simply will not do.

On the other hand dealing with a death is different from being in a relationship with a person who's married, have commitment problems or trying to understand why the relationship isn't working. But then again, I might be wrong.

My girls have been by my side every step of the way, and even suggested I move into a new house and start over without so many memories of the life Marcus and I shared there.

After taking a hiatus from my business I couldn't wait to get my patients, again; which, I hoped would numb the pain. I quickly realized how bad of an idea that was.

My clients rely on and pay me good money to help them resolve and fix problems. And I would not be doing them a good service if I spaced out during a session or decided at any given moment to shed a few tears. So, I had my assistant reach out to all my clients and future prospects by telling them I would be out of the office a little longer and will reschedule in due time. I also provided a list of therapists I knew and highly recommended for them in the event they needed to seek help while I was away.

Some of my clients heard about Marcus's passing and sent me cards, flowers and small trinkets to show solace. All of the well wishes were nice, but it wasn't enough. To make matters worse, Mr. and Mrs. Ingram checked on me weekly as we promised to be of support to each other until our hearts healed.

I stayed in bed all day, barely eating and forget about personal grooming. I couldn't even go into my bathroom without feeling his presence, the smell of his colognes and sometimes I thought I heard his voice at night. Maybe I was losing my mind? Or is he trying to tell me something? Whatever it was I didn't want to hear it, and only wanted to be left alone.

"Wake your ass up, get up out this funky bed and, please, for the love of God, wash your ass!"

The voice sounded familiar; but, it was all a blur because once again I drank a whole fifth of Hennessy. Nivea had been beyond patient with me, and once again playing the role of aunty/ mommy for Sydney to give Demoni a break (as she was now a full-fledged teenager). God, where had the time gone?? As of January 28, 2015, she said she had had it with me and was not going to lose me, too, of a broken heart. If I could count on anyone keeping it real with me, it was her.

She opened my blinds, immediately started ripping my bed apart replacing sheets, pillows and comforter with a new and clean set.

"Now, while I start the laundry and make up your bed, go take a shower."

She gave me the greatest hug and kiss on my forehead because my breath reeked of alcohol. All I could do was comply. I gained enough strength to undress myself and let the water from the shower submerge my body to a new and clean me. I cried and cried, which seemed like forever but was really only 20 minutes. I managed to comb the knots out of my hair and put it in a neat bun, brushed my teeth and headed back to my room to figure out what was next for me in my life.

"Thank you, Nivea, for coming over here and making me get up."

"You're welcome, girl. You are my sister and I will always be here for you…no matter what."

"Hello. is anyone here"? I thought I heard a door close and what sounded like people coming up the stairs of my house.

"Who's that, Niv?"

She looked at me with a deviant grin that is often displayed by children. Is that Selasi? It was Selasi, Erica, Nikki and my good friend Netise – all here to help me out of this sinkhole.

"I've got movies, love, and a few bottles of wine", Erica said. We all laughed at the wine part as if I needed anymore to drink, joined together in a group hug and went downstairs.

Once I got down there, a few more surprises were waiting on me. Balloons, a table full of food and my mother was also here to greet me.

"Hey, suga! Daddy sent me over here to check on his baby girl and kicked me out the house because it's football season."

"Oh, Lord. How is Daddy?"

She gave me that look of disgust in a joking sorta way, kissed me like she used to when I was little and said daddy was fine. Just getting old and set in his ways. My parents have had tons of ups and downs but they still loved one another deeply and never gave up on each other, in spite of the drama they've encountered with infidelity.

I was so glad for the company and actually enjoyed myself. There's nothing better than friends and family during the time of need. After everyone left and I cleaned up the mess we made in the kitchen, I noticed my answering machine was blinking. So I decided I would finally check my messages and promised to get to everyone starting with Mario and Anne who were scheduled for appointments during the time of Marcus' passing. I had agreed to meet with them both free of charge.

Mario needed me the most as he still hasn't told his girlfriend about his sexual identity and I promised to include her in the next session.

The date was set and I had Mario and Trina meet at my house in the office Marcus laid out for me – the same way I had it set up at my downtown location. Working was going to be good for me, keeping me busy and taking the attention off me and onto some else.

When I opened the door, I seen the most radiant pregnant woman with long natural hair, wearing the cutest dress for a mother expecting. Mario was looking dapper, as usual, which I could see how Trina fell for him and got knocked up. Trina and I hugged it out, I congratulated her and briefly went over how I go about my sessions. She seemed a bit nervous at first, but after a cup of tea she was fine.

"Ok, let's jump right on in. I'm Dr. Porter, but you can call me Tracy. How long have you two been dating and where did you two meet?"

Trina filled me in on all the details and then I asked her if she knew why she was here. She said she sort of had an idea but wasn't quite sure.

"I think things began to shift some in our relationship when I told Mario I was pregnant. We've been distant before that; but, I just figured it was just due to our work schedules and not spending as much quality time as we did when we first started dating."

Jotting down notes, I asked Mario if that sounded accurate to him, he agreed, followed by a cough. Then I turned the floor over to Mario asking him to begin telling his girlfriend what brought them into my office today. Mario turned to Trina, rubbed her belly and grabbed one of her fat hands – a result from the pregnancy.

"You know that I love you, Trina, and I am forever grateful for you and happy about our little girl due in a few months; but, I have something to tell you that can no longer wait."

"Ok, baby, what is it?"

"I've been seeing Dr. Porter for some time now, because I am battling with something that has been affecting me since a child. First off, I was molested as a young boy by a teenaged boy who used to babysit me while my mother worked the night shift at the hospital."

"Ok, and so how does that tie me in? And why haven't you ever told me, babe? We've been together now for years."

"I know, babe, but this isn't an easy subject for a person to discuss. I wanted to tell you, but didn't know how."

Shifting in his seat, Mario let go of her hand and created some space between them. He was now going in for the kill. I moved my seat closer so that I can console either one of them, if needed. As Mario continued to tell Trina that as a result of what happened to him, he was attracted to men and been secretly seeing them off and on for a while. I suggested we take a quick break because I didn't want to put any stress on Trina or the baby.

They both agreed with me. Trina then got up breathing rapidly and rubbing her belly to keep her calm by not going into premature labor. Mario was smart by not going near her, fear of possibly being slapped. So, I decided to take over for Mario as I knew I would. I went on to explain that it wasn't Mario's fault in what happened and that most victims live in shame, guilt sometimes, struggle with their identity or are strong enough to move past it and live normal lives.

"So, are you telling me I'm not good enough, and that you don't love me anymore?" a crying Trina asked.

"No, baby, I love you so much I had to come clean, because I can't continue to lie to myself or you."

"Ok, so what else, I know there is more."

"Well, there is. I met someone, and I love him, too, and I know now I want to be with him."

Once everything was out in the open, I told Mario to leave the office so Trina and I could talk. She was hurt and felt betrayed by Mario; but, understood the deepness of the situation. She felt that had she known she would have never fallen for him as hard as she did. Now, she's stuck with having to deal with if she wanted him to be in her life at all. When Mario came back in the office Trina asked him to tell her the guy's name and to show a picture of him. And what happened next, no one in the room would have ever expected.

"Trent, huh? Let me see what he look like."

After Mario found a picture in his phone that the two of them took randomly after spin class, he handed her the phone. She studied the picture, laughed even, which seemed weird.

"Really, Trent Holloway?"

"Yeah, how do you know him?"

"I know him, Mario, real well, because he's my fucking brother! You've been fucking my brother."

Trina threw the phone at Mario and he caught it in just a nick of time; but, his face and mine were on the floor. Damn, I wasn't expecting this at all. I guess I'll be seeing more of them, and Trent, too. Man I love my job!!!

What Are You Going To Do Now, Doctor?

I woke up one night tossing and turning, pillows on the floor and clothes spread about. *"I've had enough"*, I said to myself, as if someone else was in the room. I need to find Tracy, and get back to my life, or the new one, now that I'm alone again. Marcus would be extremely upset and disappointed that I was wasting my life away. I can hear him say,

"Babe, just because my life ended doesn't mean yours is over."

Then, after I cried a river, I would go on about how part of my life is over and I feel dead without him. We would then argue about how silly that sounded, and like always he'd kiss me on the forehead and walk away. He would want me to be happy. So, just like that I opened up my laptop and booked a flight to New Orleans, Louisiana. I was reclaiming my life.

Any other time trips would be best taken with a pal or a group of friends, but this time around I have to take the journey alone. It was at that moment I realized that in order to fully heal from this hurt of losing Marcus I had to do it on my own terms without any distractions. Now that my mind was running a mile a minute, I had to pack everything I thought I'd need because I hadn't figured out just how much time I was going to need. I put on some smooth jazz, fixed me a glass of wine and went into my office to retrieve my passport that I hadn't used in a while.

Remembering I didn't intend on telling a soul until after my plane was in the air, I left both mama and daddy emails I knew they wouldn't get to until tomorrow. I decided to wait to tell Selasi and Nivea because I knew for a fact their phones would be at their hips and they would try to come with me.

Since my flight was due to leave at 7:30 am, and I wanted to beat Los Angeles early morning traffic, I arranged for my driver to pick me up at four a.m. It's been years since I've been to the Nola and as nervous as I was traveling by myself, I was also super uber excited like a kid on Christmas morning.

As I buckled up in my seat on my flight to New Orleans, I popped a piece of gum in my mouth, took out my iPod so I could listen to some music, and quickly relaxed in preparation for take-off. As I zoned out to Billie Holiday, I began to think about was me being happy again. Right now, I was in a very dark place which was not healthy.

For the last seven years in my practice I've been able to give quality advice and service and not just because I get paid to do it; but, because I enjoy helping people I've worked with. On the flip side of that, I can't seem to apply the same principles for my own life. Well, starting today all of that is going to change.

I landed in New Orleans, Louisiana at 12:30 p.m. As soon as I checked in and freshened up, I was going to hit the streets! Boy I couldn't wait and it was summertime, too, which meant, summer dresses, sandals and cute hats. I didn't have any real plans except to enjoy spending some "me" time parading around like a tourist and taking pictures. By now everyone at home knew I had snuck away and pretty soon I knew I would either receive phone calls and texts; so, I turned my phone off, at least for now. I sent everyone the same email.

"Dear love ones, it's Tracy! If you are now reading this I am on my way on a quest for healing and to get back to the 'me' we all know and love. I assure you that I'm okay and will not do anything crazy so please stay calm. I ask that you respect my space right now, and once I settle in, in New Orleans I will contact each and every one. I promise!"

I then added some extra things in each letter just for them. For example Selasi and Nivea will be joining me in Hawaii. As a way to show my gratitude for being so awesome and putting up with my dramatics, their tickets were already purchased. They just had to sort out whatever they needed to before the day of the flight. I already knew my sister would have to go shopping, as if she really needed anymore clothes; but, she was a selfie queen. Then there was Selasi, who was married and would have to arrange for the care of their youngest daughter, because her husband sucked in the daddy day care department. And even though she owned her own hair shop, she had to find a reliable employee to hold down the fort while she was away. They had a month to put it all together and I was not for any excuses.

Since I was staying at the Hilton which was next to the Superdome and only a short skip and hop from Bourbon Street, I grabbed my shoulder purse, put on my shades and blended in with my people. First stop was Oceana Grille, one of the places I've been before. I was craving some beans and rice, a Rajun Cajun Bloody Mary, turtle soup and the Blackened Redfish.

While I was people watching I had an epiphany. I would write down everything I was feeling no matter what is was as a form or way to tie it into my profession for my first seminar. But first, I had to complete this journey so that when I got home, I could write my book. Damn, I even had a title. "Look at God!"

I've been in New Orleans for nearly a week now and it's been great. Just me, my thoughts, great foods and the people of Nola. When I look back at my life and experiences, I appear to be perfect on the surface compared to the citizens of New Orleans. One of the things on my to-do list was to take a bus tour around the city, where I gained a more in-depth background about the Mardi Gras which is celebrated for two weeks just before Shrove Tuesday. The day before Ash Wednesday. I found out that this holiday began with an observance of Catholic practices and the colors purple, green and yellow stood for faith, justice and power – a flag also used by the Catholics throughout history.

New Orleans was a place where free and enslaved African settled along with American Indians sharing their cultures with the intertwining with the European settlers. This tour was led by a cool dude by the name of Tico, who explained the different architects around the city from shotgun houses and cottages to the beautiful mansions on St. Charles and the cemeteries that aren't dug 6 feet deep because of the high-water table. I made small videos and took lots of pictures of every site I visited for my memories to share and take home with me. With the mixture of cultures, great music and spicy foods, it was almost enough for a girl to stay forever.

After visiting the cemeteries a real calmness came over me and for the first time in a week, because I hadn't cried over Marcus. As I looked out the window on my way back to Bourbon Street, a rainbow appeared and all I could do was smile.

I truly believe Marcus' spirit keeps surfacing through rainbows as a way to tell me no matter how bad I'm feeling, happiness will be on the other side. I'm not quite sure how I'll ever be happy after losing him but I'm going to try hard like hell. "Mame, this is the end of the tour."

Completely startled by the interruption I almost peed on myself. "Oh, I'm sorry, my mind was elsewhere."

In his New Orleans accent Tico said, "It's, okay baby, first time here?" I told Tico that I had been to New Orleans a few other times before (before Hurricane Katrina) and I was just overwhelmed, I guess about how much had changed and what was still the same. I thanked him for the tour and exited the bus onto the streets where a live band was playing. Someone had just gotten married and there was a full-fledged parade happening in celebration of the new union. Like everyone else I, too, was filming the happy bride and groom with my phone in admiration.

"One day, Tracy, one day", I told myself. Then, out of nowhere on this sunny and humid day, it began to pour down out of the heavens. As people ran for cover, I just stood there with my arms extended allowing the drops of water to clean my body.

While everything and everyone was moving fast, I felt like I was in a Spike Lee movie, moving fast taking it all in. To the right of me was the Bombay Club on Conti Street blasting some good old Swing. Almost in a trance, I waltzed right on in and found a spot to dance. Not sure how I got a drink but what I do know is that I was feeling myself. I was free like a bird out of his cage which is different from my normal reserved self.

After about 20 minutes of grooving people dispersed from the dance floor to mingle about back to their tables. I found a place on the wall. I hadn't checked my phone in a while and when I did, I realized that it was late and I hadn't eaten since breakfast.

Also remembering I was still wet from the earlier pouring of rain and not wanting to catch a cold, I walked briskly to my room. However before I retired, I ordered since room service, took a quick shower and blow dried my hair before checking in with mom and dad. I went over the days so far with my parents for about 20 minutes, until I heard a knock at my door. "Ma, Daddy my room service is here and I'm starving. I'll call you later. Love you. Bye."

Before I hung up completely my parents managed to say a few words between them two. I devoured my shrimp Poe Boy sandwich, fries and coleslaw. Full and hung over by the day, I laid across my bed in my robe and slept like a baby.

I had one more day until my flight left New Orleans. I decided to find a place to get some quick braids, so I could be ready for the next destination. We all know how black women are about their hair in wet climates and I was no exception. After that, the plan was to hit up the mall for a few cute pieces, try my luck at the casino and shower all before the river boat dinner tour.

I had my camera and phone charging because I wanted to take pictures of all the beautiful sights New Orleans had to offer. There were single people, and young and old couples with their children on the river boat. Since I took the trip I had to admit I was feeling lonely. I knew that I was going to see my family again but seeing all the beautiful people out celebrating life made me wish I had at least one tag-along person. At the end of the day, however, I knew that I had to take this journey on my own, if I was ever going to heal. In that very moment a tear dropped, followed by a smile. The last thing I needed was for people to start looking at me funny, because I was crying in a crowded room full of great music and delicious foods.

I had an amazing time on my trip thus far; but, it was time to pack up and head to the next destination. Like kid on the first day of school, I couldn't contain myself. Since my flight was leaving early, I retired early, so I could not only pack but get a good night's rest.

All I kept thinking about while I was trying to go to sleep was how I was so ready to hit the beautiful Island of Hawaii and hang out with my loved ones, and how I think they'd be proud of me for making progress in the midst of my current despair. Being someone who hates the idea of being alone, I must admit that for the first time I'm finally learning how to enjoy my own company.

Coming out of your comfort zone isn't always easy, but it doesn't necessarily have to be hard either, if you just give it a try. Crazy how I had to load up my suitcase and travel over three thousand miles to find that one. Even if I spent money on flights, hotels and so forth, what I can take away now is that you are in control of how you want your life to be, no one else.

On my flight from New Orleans to Honolulu, Hawaii, I had yet another one of my many epiphanies. As my mind was stirring up a big pot of gumbo, I also decided that in my first speaking engagement, I was going to divulge about mental health, relationships, my personal journey and how I can help my community. I realized that Marcus' death was not just about me, but anyone who's lost a loved one.

I also decided I was going to add a support group to my business and hire a few people in the field who can be of great service for me dealing with different issues. It would be free, of course, and I would pay my counselors out of my own pocket. If the Lord can bless me with a beating heart and air to breathe, I can be a blessing for others.

I jotted down some notes, happy faces, ideas, venues for the seminar and places I could look for the help I was going to need for the support groups. I was beyond excited! For one, being able to afford to travel, include my support team in everything concerning my life, and the gift God gave me to be a giver without a second thought.

After checking in and freshening up a bit, I heard a few knocks on my door. I wasn't expecting Selasi and my sister for another hour, so I wasn't quite sure who'd be at my door. I threw something on really quick. "Just a minute." I didn't even check the peephole; but, I did however open the door slowly...and who did I see?!! "Mama, what are you doing here? Did you bring Daddy?"

"Well, hello to you, too. Did you miss me? And no, this is a ladies' trip only!" Coming down the hall being loud of course was my sister Nivea and Selasi. Then, right behind them running was my big baby, Sydney, I was beyond overjoyed. Oh, how much I missed my daughter and was super proud of her for being mature and understanding that mommy was not well. I hugged her so long she almost melted. The whole room was now filled with an exorbitant amount of emotions. I couldn't believe these heffas tricked me.

Although not a big fan of surprises, this is one time I'd say I was okay with it.

"Omg, I'm so glad you all made it safely here to celebrate life with me and my new beginnings."

We all took turns talking and catching each other up for over an hour, until Nivea said she was hungry and Selasi asked where the cocktails were. We all laughed simultaneously because we were thinking the same things but we let our talk and laughter get away from us, losing track of time.

So, since I had already regrouped it took the girls a few minutes to do the same and out of our private villa we went. The air was clean, the people were super friendly and willing to help us get around. We found a quaint restaurant called Da Poke Shack, where they served the best fish and other seafood I've had ever in my life. They also had salads, sides, tasty drinks and even great gluten-free options for those on special and restricted diets. After we had lunch, we got the itis of course and all agreed to go back to the villa and take a nap until the festivities began later that night.

I woke up rejuvenated and the happiest I've been in months. I was thankful for being alive and also blessed to have family and friends who love and support me, despite my flaws. After dinner the girls and I regrouped and went dancing at one of the local clubs, which was a lot of fun. I opted to leave a little early so that I could spend some one-on-one time with Sydney and catch up on so much that I know I've missed. All in all, I felt brand new, reborn, fresh to start over with a clean slate as though I had never known what it felt like to be broken hearted.

After Sydney settled in for the night, the girls and I had drinks, partied with the locals and took plenty of pictures to add to our many trips to come. Even my mom dropped it like it was hot a little. "Okay, mom, don't overdo it trying to hang with us young folks."

"Girl, hush, I was dropping it before you were even thought of, and plus, I haven't been out in a while."

"I heard that, Mrs. P", Selasi said. Everyone was laughing while I was asking them to not encourage her, because once she started, we'd never hear the end of it. Even my sister agreed with me on that one.

"If you girls are lucky, I just might school you on some things."

"Ugh, mom really…not today. Or ever please."

"Tracy, how do you think you and your sister got here? Shoot, depending on how I feel when I get back to Los Angeles, I just may have enough to give your daddy a little taste." I no longer wanted this conversation to keep rolling, so I caused a diversion and headed for the bar for more rounds of drinks. For a quick second everything got quiet, even with all the noise around me. In my inebriated state, I said a quick prayer thanking God for allowing myself to let go and live for me.

We stayed in Hawaii for five glorious days and as much as I didn't want the party to end, I was actually happy about going home to my new home I purchased two months ago. I wasn't 100% about leaving my first home (because of all the great memories there); but, it was time. Now I am.

People say you only get one soulmate during a lifetime, and I believe that to be true. Although my experience with love was short-lived, I'll never forget it as long as I remain on this earth. I remember when my mom found out I was pregnant, she tried to have "the talk" with Nivea and I (which was too late for me); but, she went on and on for an hour about how we had time for boys and how we should never trust a word they say, because they all wanted one thing. She went on to say Demoni lied to me about saying he loved me because if he really did, he wouldn't have gotten me knocked up.

That trauma hurt me for years and I guess a part of me never got over that. "The only men you can trust is God and your father," my mom said.

Some people get involved in relationships for various reasons, but at the end of the day one should never lose sight of who they are. I tell my clients all the time that after a breakup it's ok to be single for a while, to re-evaluate sometimes and get in touch with themselves. Not that breaking up doesn't affect us; but, it's important to remember that you had a life before that person entered your life and it will continue on after them.

Women especially fall victim in feeling as though they aren't good enough, unless they have a man and often think they need a man's validation. News flash, ladies. You don't! You are strong, beautiful, important and valued – all on your own, just the way you were made. If you think a man makes you, then you are crazy and in need of some serious help. Like my mom told me many moons ago, "You are all the love you need".

My life has taken me on some dangerous rides, and some good and bad turns; but, I wouldn't change them for the world. They have made me who I am, allowing me to share my journey with people who need encouragement, guidance and constructive criticism. Moving forward I'm going to practice what I preach and see how things change for me. I can't promise I'll go back to being the old Tracy, falling head over heels in love again; but, what I will do is love "me" more every day. And as far as dating goes, well a girl has her needs; but, I'm not rushing into anything unless I get a sign from God himself.

As always, "Peace, love and eateries."

About The Author

G.C. Tindley is a new and upcoming author from Long Beach, California, who now resides in Marietta, Georgia. At an early age she knew she was going to be an English teacher; but, God had other plans. Even with earning her Masters Degree in Education from Ashford University, her passion for writing was much too strong to shake. Taking a leap of faith, she decided to pursue her dreams and live life on her terms, for once.

Tindley is a city girl who enjoys family time, cooking, all types of music and watching old, black and white movies. If you enjoyed reading this book, be on the lookout for her next project, *"Kitty's Midnight Tales."*

Other Books to Enjoy:
www.TheSolidFoundationGroup.com

Pieces of Her Life
by G.C. Tindley
Genre: Fiction / Erotic Fiction

Live Every Moment
by Shatanese Reese
Genre: Autobiography/ Inspirational

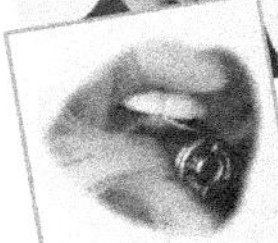

Bullet Proof
by Bodie Quinette
Genre: Christian Non-Fiction / Self-Help

A Portrait of Virginia A. Smith
by Virginia A. Smith
Genre: Memoire / Inspirational

Poetic Motifs' Significance of 9
by Kish Andes
Genre: Poetry

How To Fade Like Griffin
by Kendrick Henderson
Genre: Trade / Educational

The Pig Who Became President
By Alana Johnson
Genre: Children's

Set Free by Truth
By Amari Johnson
Genre: Children's / Science Fiction

CheckMate
by Lex
Genre: Urban

The Cartel's Daughter Unedited
by Carmine
Genre: Urban

All are Available in Paperback or E-Book Formats

Anywhere Books Are Sold*

* Your online review for any of the listed books will be greatly appreciated.

To learn more about the authors and/
or their upcoming books |or| to obtain
information about becoming an author
yourself, please visit our website:

www.TheSolidFoundationGroup.com